The Boy Kelsey

The Boy Kelsey

a novel

ALFRED SILVER

GREAT PLAINS
TEEN FICTION

Great Plains Teen Fiction
(an imprint of Great Plains Publications)
420–70 Arthur Street
Winnipeg, MB R3B 1G7
www.greatplains.mb.ca

Great Plains Publications gratefully acknowledges the financial support provided for its publishing program by the Government of Canada through the Book Publishing Industry Development Program (BPIDP); the Canada Council for the Arts; as well as the Manitoba Department of Culture, Heritage and Tourism; and the Manitoba Arts Council.

Design & Typography by Relish Design Studios Ltd.

Printed in Canada by Friesens Printing

LIBRARY AND ARCHIVES CANADA CATALOGUING IN PUBLICATION

Silver, Alfred, 1951-
    The boy Kelsey / Alfred Silver.

ISBN 978-1-894283-89-2

    1. Hudson's Bay Company—Juvenile fiction. 2. Northwest, Canadian—Juvenile fiction. I. Title.

PS8587.I27B69 2009   jC813'.54   C2008-906925-0

Mixed Sources
Cert no. SW-COC-001271
© 1996 FSC

FSC

ENVIRONMENTAL BENEFITS STATEMENT

Great Plains Publications saved the following resources by printing the pages of this book on chlorine free paper made with 100% post-consumer waste.

TREES	WATER	ENERGY	SOLID WASTE	GREENHOUSE GASES
10	3,509	7	451	845
FULLY GROWN	GALLONS	MILLION BTUs	POUNDS	POUNDS

Calculations based on research by Environmental Defense and the Paper Task Force.
Manufactured at Friesens Corporation

A Note to the Reader

SOME HISTORY BOOKS WILL TELL YOU Henry Kelsey was born in 1667, some in 1670, either one of which would make him a few years older than I have him in this story. Honest history books will tell you nobody really has a clue when Kelsey was born. And I'm here to tell you that in those days apprentice boys started very young.

Now Reader Read for I am well assur'd
Thou dost not know the hardships I endur'd

For many times I have often been opprest
With fears & Cares yt I could not take my rest
Because I was alone & no friend could find
And once yt in my travels I was left behind
Which struck fear & terror into me
But still I was resolved this same Country for to see

The Inland Country of Good report hath been,
By Indians but by English yet not seen
Therefore I on my Journey did not stay
But making all ye hast I could upon our way

—Henry Kelsey

I

ON THE ROCKY GREY SHORE of Hudson Bay in the spring of 1690, "the boy Kelsey" sat trying to convince a native fire-making machine to work in his hands. Henry Kelsey didn't much like being called "boy," but he was still a few years short of being officially a man and he was just plain short, even for his age. As long as The Company could keep on calling him "boy" they could keep on paying him apprentice wages. The one and only Company: The Governor and Company of Adventurers Trading into Hudson's Bay. But it hadn't been "boy" a couple of months back, when one of The Company's officers had foolishly gone for a walk outside the fort at the time of year when polar bear mothers take their cubs out onto the bay ice for the first time. Then it had been just plain: *"Kelsey! Help!"*

A wisp of smoke feathered out of the fire-maker. Kelsey leaned forward to blow the baby spark into flame, and ended up blowing it out. Try again. The fire-maker truly was a brilliantly simple invention, or so it seemed to Kelsey, like so many of the devices the natives had come up with to live in their land. It was a kind of miniature bow and arrow, except with much too long a bowstring and the arrow fired sideways.

You wrapped the bowstring around a pointed piece of stick, pressed the point down on a flat piece of wood and held the top of the stick down with a hollowed-out bit of stone in your left hand while your right hand worked the bow back and forth, spinning the drill-stick. The grinding of wood on wood ground out a black, smoky powder that would eventually spark. Eventually...

Kelsey had snuck outside the fort to do his practicing, because the men he worked for would call him a fool-child for playing with such primitive nonsense. After all, you could start a fire much more easily with flint and steel and a pinch of gunpowder. But what if you didn't have flint and steel and a pinch of gunpowder? What if your boat had overturned on a wilderness river, and all you had left were your shivery wet clothes and your belt knife? What then?

They would've found that question even more ridiculous than an apprentice laddy playing with an Indian's fire-starter toy. They never ventured farther outside the fort than they could walk back before sunset—except during the week or so once a year when the supply ships hove in and anchored on the bay, and even then, the boats ferrying furs out and supplies in were never out of sight of the fort.

The soft whirring and grinding of the fire machine was suddenly blotted out by the boom of a cannon. Kelsey was so tightly concentrated on what he was doing that the thunderclap jolted his head and hands up and he dropped the stone and the bow. He laughed at himself. It was only the noon gun, which meant it was time for him to get back to the fort and the mess hall and then back to work. Work would probably be something like wrestling the same barrel of axe heads from the south warehouse to the north warehouse he'd moved it from last summer. But, for a fatherless boy grown up on the

back streets of London, any kind of work that put food in
his mouth and clothes on his back was worth the doing. He
could do a lot worse than being an apprentice in a trading
company that was barely older than he was. The Company of
Adventurers had no sons-of the sons-of the founding fathers
to perch their fat rumps on the rungs of the ladder to becoming a Chief Trader someday, or even a Chief Factor.

Kelsey stashed his fire-maker in the cranny between two
rocks and headed back toward the log-walled fort, properly
called York Factory. He had to zigzag his way between other
log walls—or semi-walls—planted on the slope between the
shore and the fort in case a French or Dutch ship sailed into
the bay and The Company's men wanted closer-range cover
to shoot at landing parties.

At the top of the slope were a couple of birch bark wigwams put up by the first batch of inland natives to canoe
down-river from the west to trade at the bay this year. The
Home Indians, the ones whose territory York Factory was
built in, didn't much like the inland tribes. But The Company
had told the Home Indians that if they wanted to keep on getting guns and knives and hatchets, they couldn't use them on
the Indians who brought all those lovely, thick, rich, glossy
inland furs down to the bay. Rich furs, rich fur traders.

A scar-faced man with an eagle feather in his hair flicked
his black eyes in Kelsey's direction as Kelsey passed by the
wigwams. The eyes didn't look particularly friendly and the
scars under the left one were three parallel lines running
straight down his cheek, like he'd been clawed by a lynx—not
exactly a cheery-mornin' face. Nonetheless, Kelsey nodded
at him and said, "Wachiye."

The eyes and the scars didn't twitch, but the mouth below
them grunted back, "Wachiye," which reassured Kelsey he

must've pronounced it close to right. Kelsey knew that The Company's officers at York Factory were impressed with his remarkable ability to pick up the native languages. Kelsey also knew that he'd actually picked up about as much as the average two-year-old Indian child, but if the officers wanted to think him remarkable, he wasn't going to correct them.

Outside and beside the fort gates there was a red blanket laid out on the ground. At one end of it sat a red-bearded Company trader beside a stack of trade goods. At the other end sat a couple of natives beside a stack of beaver pelts. All the trading happened in the open air, or in sheds outside the fort, because no natives were allowed inside the fort. Kelsey thought it a foolish and troublesome rule, but wise apprentice lads didn't go quibbling out loud about company policy.

The noon meal in the servants' mess was a watery mess of a stew that tasted like it might have a few bits of seagull in it or the tail ends of an old walrus. But at least it was something warm and wet to soften the hardtack biscuits in. The Officers' Mess was no doubt serving something like fresh venison brought in by the Home Guard, as the Home Indians were called. Kelsey didn't think about whether the difference was fair or unfair, he just thought about taking his own meals in the Officers' Mess some day.

As the servants' mess was clattering with empty dishes being cleared away, one of the junior officers stuck his head in the door to shout over the din, "The boy Kelsey is wanted by the Governor. Now."

The stew and hardtack coagulated in Kelsey's stomach. As he crossed the courtyard to the log house where the fort governor held court, he wondered what he might've done wrong, or hadn't done right. The supply ship was due in a few weeks, so if the Governor was fed up with him, the apprentice boy could easily be shipped back to England. Back to what? Maybe a job scraping the open sewer gutters on the streets of London, if he was lucky. Kelsey was still an indentured servant, meaning that his pathetic wages still hadn't paid off what he owed The Company for his passage from England and his room and board and clothing and practical education. If The Company dumped him on the dock, he'd have nothing but a bad reputation.

The Governor was sitting in a large chair set back from a large table where a clerk was scritching a quill pen across a large piece of paper. The Governor's curled black wig hung down past the shoulders of his gold-buttoned green velvet coat. The Governor said, "Ah, Kelsey, sit ye down, lad," and pointed at a stool beside the table. "Would ye care for a mug of beer?"

Kelsey wasn't unaccustomed to drinking beer. One mugful was served out to every servant with the noon meal, and two with supper. If he was going to get another one today on top of his rations, he wasn't going to argue. "Yes, sir. If you please, sir." The offer did suggest the Governor wasn't unhappy with him. Then again, maybe what the Governor had to say was going to be so bitter to swallow Kelsey was going to need a mug of beer to wash it down.

A servant brought a pewter tankard. Kelsey sipped cautiously, trying not to get bubbles up his nose. The Governor said, "The Company is prospering, Kelsey, but not as much as it should, or could. And the bedemmed French down south are getting dem cheeky about pushing north and west to steal our trade.

"At present, York Factory is the only trading post we have for the natives to bring their furs to. But even before the bloody Frenchies snuck up and burned Moose Factory and drove our people out of James Bay, we were still getting only a fraction of what is out there. And no one knows exactly what is..." the Governor inclined his head to the west, toward the wilderness York Factory was perched on the edge of, "...out there." The Governor pasted on a smile to show that what might be out there didn't terrify him in the least, not really, not at all. "Ahem. But ye, Kelsey, ye've travelled inland before, and in the company of a native."

"Well, yes sir, but that didn't, um, turn out so well." The summer before, Kelsey and a boy of the Home Guard had been sent north to scout out other river inlets where The Company might set up trading forts. They'd barely gone more than a hundred miles before Kelsey discovered that the other boy truly was just a boy. Either the Indian boy had lied about how good a guide he could be, or was scared witless of meeting up with Eskimos, or both. Kelsey'd eventually had to give up in disgust and turn back for York Factory.

"And, sir, on that trek we were never often inland enough to be out of sight of the bay. So I don't really know any more about what's 'out there' than you do." As soon as that was out of Kelsey's mouth, he realized it might sound cheeky to suggest there was anything an apprentice boy might possibly know more than a fort governor about anything, so he added, "Sir."

"Nonetheless, ye've proven yerself capable of undertaking such an...undertaking."

For some reason, undertaking put Kelsey in mind of undertaker. This was starting to feel strange. Governors didn't have these kinds of conversations with apprentice-boys. Governors didn't have any kind of conversations with them, except, "Good job, lad," or "Stand up straight."

"The party of inland natives who are here now," the Governor went on, "speak of another tribe west of them, the Naywatamee Poets..."

Kelsey had no idea what *Naywatamee* might mean. He did know that *Nayak* could mean "the edge" or "the border" or "the hem" depending on what other pieces of words it was combined with. The Indian language didn't combine separate words into sentences like English did, but joined up pieces of words with other pieces to make combination words. As for *Poets*, just about all the natives were fanciful or poetical to an English way of thinking—chanting songs around their campfires outside the fort because the Northern Lights were dancing, or because they weren't. Or maybe the Naywatamees truly were makers of poems like some tribes were makers of fishnets, or maybe not. Or maybe "poets" was just the way an English ear misheard an Indian word, or maybe not. Kelsey wasn't about to ask a Governor to explain himself.

"The Naywatamee Poets are said to have a great wealth of beaver pelts, and they live in the land of the buffalo..."

Kelsey had never seen a buffalo, and neither had any other white man. He'd thought he'd seen one on the failed trek north last summer, and he'd shot it for provisions. But when he'd got back to York Factory and compared a scrap of its pelt to a buffalo pelt in the warehouse, the long straight hair of the creature he'd killed was nothing like the buffalo's thick curls. Somebody'd told him his beast must be one of the musk oxen reported by ships searching for the Northwest Passage.

"The Naywatamee Poets, however, do not know we are here and that we have many wonderfully useful things to trade for their furs. Or perhaps they do know, but have no idea of how to find us. Or perhaps they do have some idea, but are afraid to travel through another tribe's territory. Whichever, it is a very unfortunate situation for them, and for us."

Kelsey didn't have a ghost of a clue why the Governor was telling him all this, so he just nodded. The Governor took a silver snuffbox out of his waistcoat pocket, flicked up the lid and started to tap out a pinch but stopped himself and held the shiny little box out towards Kelsey. "D'ye take snuff, Kelsey?"

"Um, no, sir, thank you, sir." Kelsey didn't know if that was the proper way for an apprentice-boy to respond to a Governor offering him his snuffbox, since such a thing had never been known to happen.

"Good lad—filthy habit. Bright young pup like ye shouldn't be fouling his sniffer." The Governor tapped a pinch of snuff powder out onto his left hand, sniffed it up and gave a little sneeze, then tucked the box away. "Ahem. Well, to the point. You see, Kelsey m'lad, there is a way to resolve that unfortunate situation for the Naywatamee Poets, and for us. The batch of inland Indians who are camped outside our gates now have agreed that if one of our men is willing to go with them, they will take him back to their home country and escort him onward to the land of the Naywatamee Poets.

"If one of our men is brave enough to volunteer to go with them, he could also keep a journal of the distance and direction travelled each day, and a description of the country. Ye did a dem excellent job of that on yer...unfortunate expedition last summer. This expedition would take a year at least, perhaps two—our man would have to winter in the wilderness with the natives, of course, and return here with them in the spring."

Kelsey had enough sense to not say: "Why wait till spring?" or let his face show he was wondering why, since the Governor seemed to assume he would know. He did know that the inland Indians always started showing up at York Factory in late May or early June and were gone by the start of July. He'd never asked himself why, but it must be so they could get back home before the rivers froze. No inland Indians wanted to be stuck at York Factory for the winter, especially as they were not allowed inside the fort and were not welcomed by the Home Guard. If the Governor's brave volunteer wanted to come straight back after a summer exploring, he'd have to paddle his own canoe without guides or protection.

Kelsey realized that while he'd been answering his own question he hadn't been listening to the Governor. "...but ye get along well with the natives and seem to enjoy their company. We would supply ye with a new flintlock rifle—a *rifle*, not a smooth-bore musket—and a sample selection of trade goods. The Company would be very grateful to whomever undertook this expedition, and ye seem to be just the man for the job."

Oh, now it was "man," not "boy." A number of things flicked through Kelsey's mind. One was that saying no would not be a good way to please his masters, and in this world there were only masters and servants. Another thing was that a year or two roaming around with the Indians didn't sound like a bad alternative to moving barrels from one warehouse to another. But there was one other thing, something the Governor hadn't said out loud and wasn't likely to, that made the boy Kelsey just the man for the job. Kelsey didn't fancy himself the brightest puppy in the kennel, but he wasn't a drooling idiot. It wouldn't be a crippling blow for The Company if an apprentice-boy ended up starved to death in the wilderness, or trampled by a buffalo, or pincushioned with the arrows of unfriendly natives, or dead of a thousand other possible causes that no one could imagine, because no one could imagine what was actually "out there."

Kelsey grappled onto something to say that was in between yes and no. "But, sir, an expedition like that— exploring-like—you'd want the explorer to bring back a map of what's ... out there. Mapmaking's not one of the things The Company's taught me, sir, and I don't think it's easy learned, not for maps that're useful and ... accurate-like. So maybe you need someone more—"

"Not a bit of it. All we'd need our man to bring back is a clear-writ journal and, like I said before, ye've done that before."

That twigged Kelsey to something else the Governor wasn't saying. Most Company servants didn't bother their heads with higher matters like The Company's precious Royal Charter, but Kelsey'd always had ideas above his place in life. When the King granted the Company of Adventurers monopoly trading rights to northern North America, one of the conditions was The Company's promise to explore that vast and mysterious land. Twenty years since the ink dried on the Charter, and still no reports of inland exploration for the King. Good chance His Majesty was getting a tad impatient. Someone who brought back a journal of proof to show to the King would be taking a big step toward the officers' mess.

"Well, 'twould be even better," the Governor went on, "if besides the journal our man also brought back some canoes full of Naywatamee Poets to trade with us, and even better even would be canoes full of..." He swivelled his curly wigged head to gaze out the window to the west. "'Tis said that even farther westward, beyond the Naywatamee Poets, are the Assinae Poets—a fierce and fearsome people who dominate the tribes around them and hence have all the best trap lands. They are strong in their own lands, but carrying valuable commodities through an enemy tribe's territory is another kettle. If our man could find the Assinae Poets, and make a peace between the tribes so the Assinae Poets could bring their furs to us..."

The Governor went dreamy-eyed, maybe seeing images of faraway lands, or maybe pots of gold. Then he focused on Kelsey again. "So, Henry, m'lad, d'ye think ye're brave enough to volunteer?"

Kelsey pondered a brief moment on the difference between brave enough and fool enough, then said, "When do I start, sir?"

II

MEYOKWAIWIN SLIPPED SIDEWAYS from between the rabbit blanket and bulrush mats she shared with her little sisters, pulled her deerskin dress on over her head and stooped out of the wigwam. She walked down through the dew toward the river, rubbing sleep-sand out of her eyes. Her family didn't always camp beside a river with such low banks, where she could stumble down to the water half-asleep without a good chance of falling over a rock ledge and breaking her neck. So she didn't like to waste mornings like these by staying in bed till everybody else was getting up and clattering around.

She knelt beside the river to scoop cool water up over her face, but before bending forward, she flurried her hands back and forth to ripple the surface of the water so it wouldn't show her face back to her. Because she knew what she would see if it did. She would see a face that was flattened in on one side. The left side was a perfectly ordinary face, but the right side, under the eye, was a straight slope from the jawline up to the mid-line of her nose, like a clay doll someone had stepped on when it was still wet. She'd heard stories of a faraway tribe called the Flatheads, who kept a slanted board tied tight to the foreheads of girl children because they thought a woman with a sloped-back forehead looked good. But that was on purpose, and the same for every woman in the tribe, so none of them looked funny.

No one remembered exactly how Meyokwaiwin's face had got mashed flat on one side, except that it had happened when she was still a baby with soft bones. Well, everyone remembered exactly how it had happened, but remembered different things. One remembered that her cradleboard had fallen out of a tree and hit a flat rock, someone else remembered that a caribou who wasn't quite dead had kicked back when she was crawling past, another remembered that someone overexcited in a scalp dance had swung his spear too wide...

Sometimes she thought it cruel that they called her *Meyokwaiwin*, which meant "pretty face." But then, her mother had a very scrawny sister called Bear Fat. And names could change. Meyokwaiwin's father, Morning Wolf, had once been Short Eyes. Meyokwaiwin might turn out to be only her girl-name, and she was almost a woman.

The cold water on her face washed the sleep out of Meyokwaiwin's eyes, and her head. Without looking down, she scooped up another bit of river in the cup of her hand and brought it to her mouth. The fresh water, with a slight taste of spruce and cold stone, washed the sleep out of her mouth and throat. She could hear the rest of the camp waking up behind her: her father and his brother and a friend and their wives and children. So she stood up to go back, but something on the other side of the river caught her eye, something worrisome.

Among the dark green of the trees with needles and the lighter greens of the trees with leaves, there was a flicker of yellowy-brown. But when Meyokwaiwin squinted she could see it was only a bow tree, so called because their wood was the best for making bows. Bow trees were always the first to lose their leaves, and the last to get them back, so their changing colour didn't mean the seasons would change soon. The Rivers Freeze Moon was still a ways off, not until after The Moon When The Deer Rub Their Horns and The Moon When The Geese Fly.

Back at camp, Meyokwaiwin helped her mother and her father's second wife make a soup out of the fish the men had speared by torchlight last night. It took awhile. Once the three biggest birchbark rogans had been half filled with chopped fish and water, and dried herbs from Meyokwaiwin's mother's pouches, the soup had to be cooked. The only way to do that was to heat rocks in the campfire, then carefully pick them up with two strong sticks and lower them even more carefully, so that the hot rocks went down into the soup without touching the birchbark. It *was* possible to cook soup over the fire on a grill of green sticks, but you had to keep a worried eye on whether any tongues of flame were licking higher than the level of soup in the rogan and reaching the dry birchbark above, or whether the grill was starting to smoulder.

Meyokwaiwin had once seen a miraculous, big black pot that could actually be sat right onto a fire with no worries. It belonged to a woman whose family hunting territory was farther toward the sunrise than Meyokwaiwin's. It had come from far away, traded down the line from the mysterious, white-faced men who camped on the edge of the salt water where the sun rose. Meyokwaiwin's mother had naggled at her father that life would be much easier if they had a pot like that, too. Morning Wolf had said that the only way that could happen was if he went away for a whole summer, to make his way to the salt water and back. Meyokwaiwin's mother had looked thoughtful at that.

Meyokwaiwin had understood what her father was saying, about going all the way to where the pots came from instead of trading for one that came their way. Every hand something passed through made it cost more. The copper bracelets that came from way up in Eskimo country could probably be had up there at ten for one fox pelt, but by the time they'd travelled down to where Meyokwaiwin lived it was more like *two* for one. Meyokwaiwin had seen her father trade one bracelet to a man farther south for the same as her father had traded for three.

Her father had a wondrous iron knife—not any sharper than a good flint knife but not as brittle and unlike flint it could be sharpened when it grew dull—that he'd bought for two beaver pelts, which might've bought him *ten* knives at the place where the white-faced men camped. So a big heavy iron pot that'd passed through as many hands as the knife had, and been carried as far, would probably cost all the furs Morning Wolf could trap and hunt in a whole winter. And the family would have to live on weasel and fox and beaver meat all that winter, because spending all his days getting so many fur animals would mean he wasn't hunting caribou or deer.

The fish soup in the birch bark pot was just starting to steam when a sharp, startling boom cracked the air. Meyokwaiwin looked up at the sky. There were no storm clouds there, and she called herself an idiot for looking up —the sound hadn't been deep enough or rumbly enough for thunder. It was a gun. Meyokwaiwin had seen and heard a gun before. At The Gathering last spring, when all of the wandering, small bands and families came out of the deep woods where they'd wintered, a man from the Whispering Lake country had had a gun and had fired it at a tree to show it off.

This gunshot seemed to've come from a little ways down-river, around the bend to the left of the camp. The three men of the camp, and their older sons, grabbed their bows and stood looking in that direction, with arrows nocked. The women and older girls grabbed babies and stood huddled behind the men, waiting to see if they should scatter into the woods. Around the bend came a long canoe with four men paddling, and then another and one more.

Meyokwaiwin's father took the arrow out of his bow and said, "If they meant to kill us and rob us, they wouldn't come so out-in-the-open where we could pick them off before they got to shore. And if they meant to just pretend to be friendly until they got in among us, they wouldn't've fired off a gun."

Meyokwaiwin put down the baby brother she'd snatched up, and everyone in the camp changed from worrying about the men in the canoes to wondering about them. Morning Wolf had a knack for seeing "if this, then that," or "if that, then this," and he never saw wrong in things that mattered. Along with that proven knack, his hook nose gave him the look of Ohoomisew, the Great Horned Owl, who sees things that are dark to others. It was well-known that people who listened to Meyokwaiwin's father generally found themselves in deep water less often than people who didn't, so people generally did—except maybe for Meyokwaiwin's mother.

As the canoes came closer, Meyokwaiwin could see that there was a man in the middle of the lead one who wasn't pad-dling, and was wearing a very strange kind of hat, or hood. At first she thought it might be made of copper, but the colour wasn't quite right, more like the bow-tree leaves she'd seen that morning. Then as the canoes were beached and the man stepped out, she saw it wasn't any kind of hat or hood, it was his hair. He must be one of the white-faced men from the faraway salt water. Maybe living so near to where the sun rose was what made his hair that colour.

His face wasn't exactly white, though, but a paler and pinker red-brown than the other men from the canoes. Unlike any other man she'd ever seen, he wasn't wearing a loincloth and leggings; his clothing from his waist to down past his knees was all one baggy-legged piece. All of his clothing was made from something like a thinner version of a blanket. Some people at The Gathering had had blankets, and all the women of other families envied them, because blankets were so much easier to wash clean and didn't need all the work it took to turn animal hides into soft leather.

As the men from the canoes and the men of the camp greeted and explained to each other, Meyokwaiwin learned that the sunny-haired man's name was something like "Kensey," but had a strange sound in the middle that her ear couldn't translate into anything her mouth could form. She learned that the other men from the canoes were helping him in a long journey to find the people who lived in the buffalo lands beyond the forest. And she learned, by the lightness of Kensey's voice and the smoothness of his face, that this white-faced man actually wasn't quite a man yet, maybe no older than she was. He had a kind of strange way of speaking, but all the men from the canoes sounded different from what she was used to.

The strangest thing about Kensey, though, was his eyes. They weren't dark brown, but pale blue. Meyokwaiwin tried to tell herself, for the sake of not looking at a stranger's face they way strangers looked at hers, that it was only natural that someone with hair the colour of the sun should have eyes the colour of the sky. But his eyes were too pale for that. She'd seen milky-blue eyes before, on a wolf, but she'd thought that was only because it was dead. No way around it, this Kensey had the eyes of a dead wolf or a live fish.

Meyokwaiwin's father explained to the men from the canoes that the edge of the woodlands and beginning of the buffalo lands was only a few days farther toward the sunset, but this river didn't turn in that direction. He told them the only way to get there from here was on foot, but it would be wise to wait a few days before starting out. The biting flies and mosquitoes in the deep woods were thinning out as the nights grew colder, but were still swarming pretty bad. A few more cold nights would make a walk through the woods less of a torture.

Kensey seemed to think it foolish to worry about a few bugs, but the lead man of the men from the canoes—an older man with three scars like claw lines down his face—said to him, "You ever seen a caribou run crazy with biting-bugs all over him? I seen one run till he run himself to death. Better we wait."

A great many things got unloaded from the canoes. Some of them were strange, wooden things shaped something like a tree stump, but with lines down the side and iron bands around them. And there seemed to be more guns than men from the canoes. There were a lot more things than the men from the canoes would be able to carry through the woods. Kensey offered that if some of the people of the camp would help with the carrying, he would give them presents. A gun, though, was too big a present. But if someone from the camp wanted to *buy* a gun, the present would be plenty of the black powder and little round stones that made a gun work.

Meyokwaiwin's father and his brother and friend murmured with each other and decided they had enough furs cached from last winter to buy one gun to share. Meyokwaiwin's mother hissed at her father, "An iron pot for me to cook in would be too much, but not an iron gun for you to shoot?"

Morning Wolf hissed back at her, "What good's a pot without something to cook in it? I can hunt much better with a gun. Besides, did you see them unload any big cooking pots from those canoes?"

The men of the camp and the men from the canoes began to play the ring-and-spear game, and bet against each other. They would be at it all day, and maybe into the night by firelight. Meyokwaiwin's mother said the women might as well do something useful. It was the time of year for saskatoon berries and there was a clearing nearby that was covered with saskatoon bushes. So the women and girls loaded themselves down with empty pouches and full cradleboards and headed in that direction. Meyokwaiwin looked back over her shoulder—her left shoulder, not the one that would show the flattened side of her face—and saw that Kensey was standing on the edge of the excited crowd of men and boys. They were all laughing and flapping their arms and mouths around the game, except Kensey, not looking aloof but not taking part.

The clearing still showed a few blackened stumps from the years-ago fire that had made it. Around the stumps were clumps of bushy little trees, some no taller than Meyokwaiwin's waist, some higher than she could reach. They were sometimes called arrow trees, because besides growing berries their branches were some of the best for making arrows. There would've been more purply-black berries some days earlier, before the birds got at them, but there were still plenty enough to dry for the winter, and to gobble a few fresh while filling up the pouches.

It was a day of small clouds dappling the meadow with lazy shadows, and just enough of a breeze for the trees to keep up a constant whispering under the girls' and women's voices. Meyokwaiwin was reaching up toward a cluster of berries high over her head when she heard a gasp nearby and a low, rumbling sound farther off. She looked toward the gasp and saw her father's second wife staring wide-mouthed at the edge of the clearing. Meyokwaiwin looked in that direction and saw two grizzly bears ambling out of the woods. The rumble must've been a growl from one of them.

Grizzly bears always travelled alone, except mothers with cubs. These two were almost the same size, so it must be a mother with her almost full-grown cub. A mother with a cub, almost full-grown or not, was the most dangerous kind of bear there was.

While that was passing through Meyokwaiwin's mind, the rest of her was doing like all the other women and girls around her: slowly backing away while loudly chanting or calling-out any words or non-words that came to their mouths. *Okistutoowan*—Grizzly Bear—liked to stay away from loud human noises. The trick was to not sound afraid without sounding like you were making a threat or a challenge. If the bears hung back long enough for the humans to back out and leave the tasty berry patch to them, maybe everyone who'd left the camp today would live to see tonight.

The two bears came on slowly, weaving their huge heads from side to side and sniffing the air. Meyokwaiwin was just starting to believe it was going to work, that she and all the others were going to be able to get away, when a baby started crying. The sound came from the middle of the wide space between the women and the bears. Hanging from a branch of one of the saskatoon bushes almost tall enough to be a tree was the cradleboard of Meyokwaiwin's father's brother's youngest son. Whichever of his older sisters was supposed to carry him around today must've been too scared by the bears to remember.

The two bears looked toward the crying sound and cocked their sloped-down heads, as though thinking maybe there was something even tastier than berries in that tree.

Meyokwaiwin jumped forward, shouting, "Okistutoowan! I got more meat on me than him, and you can't make me any uglier than I am already!" The bears turned toward the new sound and fixed their four dark eyes on her. Their furry lips flicked open over rows of teeth as long as her fingers. There was no use running; a charging grizzly bear was faster than the fastest man alive.

There was a loud crack, like a winter tree branch snapping in the cold. The slightly smaller grizzly bear fell sideways against its mother and then down to the ground. There was a black hole in its side, a hole that quickly turned red as blood flowed out of it. Meyokwaiwin looked in the opposite direction from the hole. At that end of the clearing there was a little, rocky hill. Standing on the hill was Kensey, lowering his gun.

Meyokwaiwin looked back toward the bears. The one still standing was rearing up, roaring, not looking at Meyokwaiwin anymore but over the tops of the berry bushes and across the clearing. The mother bear didn't need to know anything about guns to know that whatever had killed her cub had come from the left side. The only creature in that direction was the one standing on that rocky hillock.

Meyokwaiwin looked back to Kensey, who was doing something to his gun. She seemed to remember that the man with the gun at The Gathering had needed a lot more time to get it ready to fire again than it took to nock an arrow. Meyokwaiwin looked to the bears again. The mother bear still stood towering and thundering, clawing at the clouds, then dropped back onto all fours but with her head still pointed toward the far end of the clearing. Okistutoowan charged.

III

KELSEY DID HIS DAMNEDEST to divorce his mind from his hands, as the bristling silver-grey monster came roaring across the clearing at him. Mind: *Lucky the Governor gave me a rifle, I never would've made that shot with a smooth-bore musket...* Hands: *Dump some powder down the barrel, then just drop the damn powder flask, don't bother stoppering it, reach into the shot pouch...* Mind: *Amazing that a creature so fat and humpshouldered can run so fast...* Hands: *Ball and patch into the barrel, ram it down...* Mind: *On the other hand, a rifle does take longer to load, ramming the lead ball down hard enough so its edges mash into the spiral rifling grooves...* Hands: *Throw down the ramrod, pull the hammer back...* Mind: *Hard to tell where best to aim when it's on a slope, coming up the hill at me...* Hands: *Just pull the damn trigger!*

Bang! Through the smoke from the exploded gunpowder, Kelsey saw the grizzly bear knocked sideways by the impact of the bullet, then fall and slide down the slope. He lowered his rifle, propped its butt on the ground and gripped both hands around the barrel to hold himself up while his heart and lungs learned how to beat and breathe again.

Suddenly there were loud male voices all around him. The men at the ring-and-spear game had heard the first gunshot, grabbed their own guns or bows or spears and come running. They were amazed that he'd been able to hit the first bear at such a distance, and even more amazed that he'd killed two grizzly bears in less time than it took them to run to the clearing from camp. They gave him a new name on the spot: *Misstopashish*, which meant "Little Giant."

Kelsey wasn't sure whether he should be pleased and puffed-up with the "Giant" part of his new name, or embarrassed that the "Little" portion would be a constant reminder that he still wasn't a full-sized man. Maybe he never would be; other boys his same age were generally bigger than he was.

As they started skinning the bears to cut up the meat and take it back to camp, Kelsey offered to give good presents to anyone who would preserve the hides for him. A lot of furs had passed through his hands in The Company's warehouses, but he'd had no practice at stretching and scraping hides, or whatever else needed to be done to turn a raw pelt into a finished fur.

Morning Wolf shook his head. "That we never do, not with a bear. We bury the skin of a bear, along with its guts and whatever else of it we do not eat. The bear is a manitou."

Even though he'd heard the word many times, Kelsey didn't entirely understand what "Manitou" meant. It wasn't exactly a spirit, or a god, or a guardian angel, but what exactly it *was* was a mystery to him. He wondered if maybe that was the point, and that was what it meant to everybody: a mystery. Obviously, though, not all Indians had the same beliefs about bears, because he'd seen many bearskins pass through York Factory: silvery-grey ones, golden brown ones, black ones and white ones. But if the Indians he currently was with wanted to believe whatever they believed for whatever reasons, Kelsey wasn't about to argue with them. If he asked them why, they would probably look at him like he'd asked why the sky was blue, and say, "Because."

When the first bear was skinned, Kelsey saw at least one reason why they might call it a manitou. With the skin off, the bear looked remarkably like a wrinkled old man, and gave the eerie impression that an old man had pulled on a magical fur suit to go roaming and rooting through the forest.

Although the fur suit had to be buried, it seemed that the hunter could keep the claws. When the first claw was put into Kelsey's hand, he looked down at it and felt a little queasy. The gleamy black, ragged-ended ripping tool was as long as his hand, and there'd been four or five of them on each front paw. If it'd taken him another three or four seconds to reload... He decided to look at something else and not think about it.

Back at camp, while the big fire-circle in front of the wigwams was being made even bigger to roast a bear feast, Kelsey noticed that one of the camp men was taking sheets of birch bark off one side of the biggest upside-down bowl wigwam and shifting it to cover the door hole. When Kelsey asked why, Morning Wolf said, "We men will eat in there, and carry our own food in. But we must make a new doorway. Bear meat cannot be brought through a door that women have passed through." Kelsey didn't ask why; he guessed the answer would be "because."

As the camp air filled with the juicy smell of slowly-sizzling bear meat, Kelsey decided to use the time before the feast to keep up with one of the tasks the Governor had set him. He went to where he'd left his coat rolled up beside the pile of trade goods, and took a pasteboard-covered notebook and a pencil stub out of the right hand pocket. Then he left the bustle of the camp to go and sit by the riverbank, picking out a handy tree to lean his back against. Usually he wouldn't write in the day's entry until evening, when the day's travelling was done, but since they wouldn't be travelling any farther today...

Came 6 miles down ye river and came upon an Indian camp...

Six miles was pitiful, even though the distances were just his best estimate. Usually it would be eighteen or twenty miles in a day, unless they got slowed down by having to carry the canoes and cargo from one stream to another or around a waterfall, or waiting out a rainstorm so heavy they would've had to do more bailing than paddling. He'd travelled a lot of miles since mid-June, but the country hadn't changed much—at least not since they'd got about a hundred miles south of York Factory and started heading westerly. It was a greener country than around York Factory, and the water seemed bluer, and the rocks and crags were more black than grey. There had been different variations on it in every mile he'd travelled—a moss-bearded boulder here, a multicoloured waterbird there—but those kinds of picturesque details weren't what The Company was interested in.

Well, what more could he say about today to show The Company they were getting their money's worth out of him?

Ye Indians say we needs must go overland from here, but needs must wait...

Kelsey was so concentrated on forming the letters well enough that someone else would be able to read them he didn't hear something moving through the brush behind him till it'd got quite close. His head jerked up and he turned to look, wondering if he'd been a fool not to bring his rifle with him.

It was the girl they called Meyokwaiwin. She sat down nearby him, to his right. Maybe it was just coincidence that sitting to his right meant the sloped-in side of her face was away from him. She didn't look at him, just looked at the river. After a moment she said, "You saved my life."

"No, the Governor did."

"The Governor?"

The word sounded awkward in her mouth, and came out sounding more like *gubbamo*. Kelsey didn't laugh. He knew that if the Indians laughed every time he mangled one of their words, he'd never finish a sentence. He said, "The Governor gave me the long-shooting gun. I never could've hit that bear with an ordinary gun. You were very brave, jumping in front of the bears."

"I think I was very crazy." She went silent again, and kept on looking straight ahead at the river, so Kelsey went back to carefully forming letters with his pencil. After he'd got a few more words down, she said, "What do you do?"

He looked up. She'd turned her head a little more toward him, though still not full-face, and was looking down toward his hands and the notebook on his knee-desk. He said, "Oh, these marks I'm making on the..." He couldn't think of an Indian word that came anywhere close to "paper" so he just said, "...paper..." and riffled the pages to show what he meant. "...say how far I've gone each day and what the country is like. So anyone who knows how to, um, see the words in here, will know."

"Couldn't you just tell them?"

"Without this I could only tell them as much as I could remember, and they would only know what they could remember of that."

She wrinkled her forehead at that, as though white men must have pretty feeble memories, and looked at the river again. Then she said suddenly, "How do you say your name? Not your new name, the name you came with."

"Kelsey."

"Ke - ruh - sey?"

"That's close enough."

"No! I want to know it right."

"Um ... 'Kelsey' ... You have to ..." Kelsey tried to think of how his mouth made the *l* sound, something he hadn't thought about since he learned to talk, any more than he thought about how to walk. "You have to, uh ... put the front of your tongue against the, uh, inside of your mouth, just above your front teeth ..." He opened his mouth wide and stretched his lips back from his teeth so she could see. "Luh ... luh ..."

She tried, but it came out more like: "Duh."

In her concentration, she'd turned her head straight toward him, apparently forgetting about hiding the ugly side of her face. Actually, Kelsey didn't find it particularly ugly, just ... different, strange. After his last two months, "different" and "strange" were just part of the landscape.

Kelsey leaned forward to look into Meyokwaiwin's wide open mouth: smooth, white teeth and coppery-pink lips framing the nubbly red underbelly of her tongue. The angle of her tongue looked to him like the tip of it was pressed against the ridge where the tops of her front teeth met her gums. "Just a little higher and farther back — not much, just a little ..." The tongue moved. "That looks right. Try it."

"Luh," came out of her mouth.

"That's right."

"Ke - luh - sey. Keluhsey. Kelsey." She giggled and grinned. "Kelsey."

"That's me." He grinned back at her.

"Meyokwaiwin!" came in a loud, sharp, female voice from the direction of the wigwams.

"Yes, Mother!" The girl stood up and said to Kelsey, "I must help with the bear fat, scrape it into rogans to keep for the winter. Good for many things."

Kelsey watched her back disappear into the riverbank brush, a back still wearing a plain and sleeveless girl's dress, not the long-sleeved, fringed and quillworked, yoke-and-skirt arrangement that the women wore. But the legs below the short dress were shaped like a woman's; not pudgy or stick-straight like a girl's, though still cross-hatched with twig scratches like a girl's.

After the girl-woman vanished into the leaves, Kelsey went back to finishing his journal entry. Just when his stomach started reminding him he hadn't eaten much since breakfast, a drumbeat started up in the camp, signalling the start of the bear feast.

Kelsey would've been more than happy to have the feast outside, around the central firepit, with nothing overhead but tree arms and sky. But it seemed the men had to eat inside the big wigwam with the new doorway. No point asking why. The hunter who'd made the kill that made the feast, namely Misstopashish — Little Giant — had to sit in the place of honour, at the head of the circle and facing the doorway. Several large, birchbark platters heaped with steaming pieces of roast bear were brought in and set in the middle of the circle. But no one reached for them, just sat staring at the meat with drooling eyes. A smaller, wooden bowl was brought in and handed around the circle, with each man just sniffing its aroma, nodding and passing it on. Actually, only halfway around the circle. When the bowl came to Kelsey, he just sniffed and nodded like the others, and was about to sadly pass it on, when he realized the next man wasn't raising his hand to take it.

It occurred to Kelsey that the mighty hunter Misstopashish was supposed to eat from this bowl only. He unsheathed his belt knife, cut a bite-sized chunk off one of the pieces of meat in the bowl, and took a tentative nibble. It was surprisingly tender—he'd been half-afraid they might actually be called gristly bears—but had a thicker taste than moose meat. Not a sour taste, though; after all, bears gorged on sweet berries and nuts all summer long.

Kelsey realized that all the men in the circle had their eyes on him, and none of them were eating. He swallowed and said, "Good. Tastes good," and they all lunged for the meat on the platters with their hands and their knives.

Kelsey overrode the *More! Now!* signals from his stomach, and ate in very small bites, chewing them slowly and pausing in between. He guessed that the men in the circle would be offended if he stopped eating before them, and he knew they would all eat three or four or five times more than he could. Not just because they were bigger. Any living Indian had lived through starvation times at one time or another, so when there was a feast to be had, they feasted.

Even after the hand-drums were brought out and the ceremonial songs and speech-stories started, the eating continued in occasional nibbles. A long-stemmed, feather-decorated pipe was lit and passed around. It wasn't just kinnikinnik mixed with the other herbs northern Indians smoked, but also some real Virginia tobacco that Kelsey had given them as a down-payment on the presents he would give them for the coming hike through the woods.

Kelsey noticed that as the pipe was passed along the circle, some men shook their heads and passed it on without taking a puff. It seemed to bring on approving nods, and even something like smiles, from the other men. So when the pipe got passed to Kelsey, he just shook his head and passed it on. The response wasn't the same as when those others had done the same. Laughter burst out all around, and shouts of "*Ho, Misstopashish, ho!*" and the man beside him slapped him on the back. Kelsey had no idea what he'd just done, except that he'd definitely gone and done whatever it was.

And he noticed something else he didn't understand. It came after nightfall, when the inside of the wigwam was only lit by red and yellow flickers from the little firepit in the centre, the firelight sunk so low that you could see the stars through the ragged smokehole up above. All the men in the circle were *hey-yah*ing in a drum chant, and Kelsey was doing his best to hum along, when he noticed that two men weren't joining in. Morning Wolf, Meyokwaiwin's father, and Clawface, the headman of Kelsey's escort crew, were leaned toward each other and murmuring out the sides of their mouths.

Morning Wolf glanced in Kelsey's direction, caught him looking at them, and abruptly straightened his back and joined in the song. Kelsey looked away and went back to trying to hum enthusiastically. But the next time he looked in Morning Wolf's direction, Morning Wolf was closed-mouthed staring into the fire. Morning Wolf was definitely pondering on something, but Kelsey couldn't fathom what it might be. It was obviously something Morning Wolf didn't want the rest of the circle to know about, especially the little white man at the head of it.

The next morning, everybody slept late. The order of the day seemed to be to lie around in the sun belching, or maybe doing something as energetic as chipping a few flakes of flint off a half-made arrowhead. Kelsey passed the time by taking inventory of his stock of iron axe heads, glass beads, woolen blankets and more. Travelling on foot instead of by canoe meant some of it would have to be left behind, and picked up on his way back. He wasn't too worried about any of it getting stolen by those of the camp Indians who stayed behind. For one thing, it was all the property of a guest, and that was sacred. For another thing, the Indians were intelligent enough to know that if they robbed someone who could bring them such wonderful things, it wasn't likely that anyone would bring them more wonderful things in the future.

Unless, of course, that someone didn't make it back alive from the land of the buffalo hunters. In which case everything would be up for grabs. In which case someone wouldn't much care about a few glass beads, or anything else for that matter.

As Kelsey weighed two bags of beads in his hands, he had to admit that he'd been as guilty as anyone of thinking the Indians gullible for their willingness to trade furs for brightly coloured beads. Especially gullible since the natives' own quillwork and embroidery was at least as splendiferous as any beadwork, and porcupine quills, moose hair and homemade dyes cost the natives nothing. But after two months of passing through hunting and fishing camps, Kelsey'd seen how the women had to soak the quills for hours to soften them and then spend more hours pulling each quill back and forth between their front teeth to flatten them — and all that before the nasty, barbed ends could be snipped off. He hadn't seen how they made the dyes to colour the quills, but he guessed it took more hours and days of hunting up the right plant roots and mineral earth to boil together in water heated by hot stones. Quill *work*, for true. It didn't seem like such a bad bargain to trade a beaver pelt for a few handfuls of beads that only needed a bit of threading to turn a drab piece of buckskin into something as elegant as the Governor's gold-buttoned coat.

It took Kelsey a while to sort his conglomeration of trade goods into two separate piles: one to go and one to stay behind. He wanted to bring enough different samples to show the mysterious Naywatamee Poets how much better their lives could be if they took their furs to the white men camped beside the salt water. But he had to balance that against how many items a dozen people could carry through the woods. It wasn't the kind of calculation apprentice-boys were trained to make, but there was no Chief Trader there to tell him how to do it.

Once Kelsey'd got that sorted out as well as he could, he went down to his river tree again, to try and think of a way to make *Travelled 0 miles today* sound less pathetic. The few times he'd had to write that into his journal before, he'd been able to truthfully add *vicious thunderstorm* or *one canoe gashed running rapids, needs must be repaired*—things that sounded a bit more manly than *needs must wait for fear of mosquito bites*. He decided it might look better if he added to yesterday's entry: *Killed 2 grizzled bears*.

The girl-woman Meyokwaiwin came and sat nearby him again, again to his right so the flat-sloped side of her face was away from him. She kept her eyes on the river and didn't say anything, as if the only reason she'd come down here today was to see if the curls of foam around the river rocks had a different message than yesterday. After awhile he said, by way of saying something, "Turned cold last night."

"But not cold enough for you."

"Uh...?"

"Not quite cold enough to make for frost. Once there's been even a little frost on the ground, the little biters will be mostly gone. Should be soon."

"Oh." He couldn't think of anything else to say about that. But it occurred to him that there was something he could say about something else, something he could ask her to explain. It was the kind of confusing little thing he couldn't outright ask any of the other Indians about, even the ones he'd been travelling with for weeks. But for some reason it felt like he could ask her. He said, "Last night, at the men's feast, I did something that, uh...or maybe *didn't* do something that... Well, it made for a lot of laughter and surprise, and I don't know why. They were passing the pipe around, and every now and then a man would shake his head and pass it on without taking a puff, and the other men would nod approving-like. So when the pipe came to me, I did the same thing, but—"

That was as far as he got, because Meyokwaiwin burst into laughter, eyes bulged with surprise, then covered her mouth with her hand and blushed. Kelsey'd noticed that Indians blushed the same as white people, except the colour was a bit more orangey than pink. She caught her breath, took her hand from her mouth and said, "Oh, Kelsey—" but another burst of giggles cut her off. She got hold of herself, straightened her back, and trained her eyes across the river as though looking at him would set her off again. "When the men pass the pipe around the circle, a man must not touch his mouth to it if one of his wives is fat with a child, or if he has...*been with* any woman the night before. So when you passed on the pipe without puffing it..."

"Oh. Um...Oh." Now Kelsey could feel a blush creeping up his own face.

"Do you have wives, Kelsey, back where you come from?"

"Where I come from, a man has only one wife."

"It must not be very dangerous where you come from."

"Uh...Why do you say that?"

"Here, it only makes sense for a man to have more than one wife, because there are so many more women than men. Oh, as many boy children as girl children get born, but men die in wars with other tribes, or a knife fight with a man of their own tribe, or a bear that won't die with the first arrow, or a fall through the ice going out to the trap-line... Lots of ways a man can die out alone in the woods. Do you have *a* wife back where you come from?"

"Um, no, I think I'm still a bit too young to be thinking of that."

"Do you still have those bear claws?"

"Uh..." Her sudden leaps from talking about one thing to a completely different one were confusing. "Yes."

"I could string them into a necklace for you. Even the buffalo hunters would pay attention to a man who wore the claws of two grizzly bears."

"Please. That would be good, if you would. Thank you." Kelsey closed his journey journal and stood up. He wasn't sure whether the mannerly thing would be to offer her a hand up, but she was on her feet already anyway. He noticed that the bumps on her chest meant the straight-cut, girl's dress wasn't going to fit her much longer. He led her to where he'd stowed his travelling gear—a cheeky chipmunk bounced out of the pile and hightailed it into the woods—and fished the bear claws out of a pouch. As she carried them away, he noticed other people in the camp glancing at him and her and smirking—or at least the Indian version of a smirk. It made him more than a bit uncomfortable, given the foolish thing he'd gone and done with the pipe the night before.

But still, when the next morning showed patches of frost on the ground, he was glad to see that one of the camp Indians readying to carry things through the woods was Meyokwaiwin.

IV

MEYOKWAIWIN STOOD LOOKING at the pile of strange things that needed carrying, and at the back-basket standing knee-high on the ground beside her. She'd made the basket last spring, when they were camped in one place for enough days to plant a circle of stiff sticks upright in the ground and slowly weave peeled stalks of basket-bush between them. Well, not exactly a circle, because she hadn't wanted this one round like most baskets but flat on the side where it would fit against her back.

Meyokwaiwin picked up two iron axe heads and laid them in the bottom of her packbasket, then rolled up one of the wonderful, fluffy blankets tight enough to fit in on top of them. She wished she could use the blanket for sleeping in along the trail, or wrapping around herself on cold mornings, but she was quite sure Kelsey meant it to be one of the presents for the buffalo people. On top of the blanket she put in a few knife blades, and an iron platter with a long handle — she wasn't quite sure what the platter was for, but guessed it was probably something the whiteface men used for a different kind of cooking and it was definitely part of the pile of things to be carried. Then she rolled up the caribou hide that would be her bed and stuffed it in tight on top.

Her tump line was already tied to the side rims of the basket, at the right length to fit her. She'd made the tump line the winter before, from a long strip of deerhide four fingers wide. The middle part was just long enough to go across her forehead, and she'd sliced both long, trailing ends lengthwise and braided them into strong rope.

Meyokwaiwin knelt down in front of the basket, put her arms through the shoulder loops, the tump line around her forehead, and stood up to try the weight. She'd carried heavier loads before. The sides of the tump line pressed her hair against the sides of her face, and most people would've left it that way because it kept their hair out of their eyes. But Meyokwaiwin pulled the right hand side of her hair out from under the braided buckskin and let it fall free, so it would at least partly cover the right side of her face.

Meyokwaiwin's mother would stay behind at the camp, along with Meyokwaiwin's father's brother, some of the children who were almost full grown and all of the little ones. The rest set off in single file through the woods, in the direction the sun travelled every day. Morning Wolf led the way, with Kelsey next and Clawface behind him. The rest of the men from the canoes were dotted along the line of carriers, except three who guarded the rear.

The men carried very little except their guns or bows. Meyokwaiwin didn't think that was unfair, just sensible. Stumbling across a mother bear with cubs wasn't the only danger, and there would be no warning-time to put down a burden and pick up a weapon. Summer was the time for raiding, when bands of men would sneak into another tribe's territory to steal and kill, take trophies, and take prisoners to make them slaves. Usually a raiding party was only a few men, who would look for a family camped alone, or lurk around the edges of a larger camp looking to pounce on people who wandered too far into the woods with too few companions. Twenty-some people travelling together in a close-together line would usually be safe. But usually wasn't always.

About all that the men in the line carried, besides their weapons and shoulder pouches, were their beds of hides or blankets, rolled up and slung across their backs. Meyokwaiwin noticed that Kelsey's bedroll was wrapped in something that was made of tight-woven threads like a blanket, but thinner and stiffer than a blanket, and plain grey-white instead of red or blue or bone-white with stripes of colour. When they camped for the night, Kelsey made his bed by first rolling that out on the ground, then laying a blanket on top of it, then laying himself onto the blanket and another blanket on top of him.

The first night's camp, there was much joking about men who'd been sitting in canoes all summer suddenly having to walk all day up and down twisty hillocks, tripping over tree roots and fallen logs. Kelsey said, "It is good to stretch your legs after all that time in canoes—and mine could do with a little stretching." All the men laughed appreciatively that Misstopashish could make fun of himself for being a *little* giant.

All except, Meyokwaiwin noticed, her father. He was looking at Kelsey with half-closed eyes and a wrinkled forehead. The manitou who told Morning Wolf "if this then that," or "if that then this," was speaking to him again. The "ifs" didn't look to be simple this time.

Halfway through the third day, Meyokwaiwin could see the light ahead changing. She'd seen it happen before, so she wasn't surprised or confused. Most of her life had been spent in the mossy, spruce woods country, where the light was soft and shadowed and the sky was just a ragged patch above the trees, or at most a blue wigwam dome above a hemmed-in meadow or lake. But she'd been out of the forest a few times before, when her father went to trade with the buffalo people.

The woman in front of Meyokwaiwin suddenly stopped. Meyokwaiwin was in mid-step and got thrown off-balance trying to keep from bumping into the woman's back. She just managed to find her footing and stop moving forward, but it ended up leaning her backward so the back of her head bumped against the bare chest of the man behind her. The whole line was stopped dead, and no one seemed to know why.

Meyokwaiwin stepped sideways to see past the line of people trying to see over each others' shoulders. Up ahead, just inside the border of forest shade, Kelsey was standing stock still like a deer who's heard something but isn't sure what. Meyokwaiwin could see that her father had taken a few strides out past the edge of the woods and then stopped and turned to look back confusedly at Misstopashish. Kelsey stood where he was a moment longer, and then slowly walked forward. Meyokwaiwin stayed standing watching him. When he stepped out of the shade, his coppery yellow hair lit up and glinted, as though the sun was welcoming its little brother.

The line started moving again, but not for long, because Kelsey only went a little ways and then stopped again. The others gathered behind him, looking sideways at each other and not saying anything. No one wanted to get between Kelsey and whatever he was listening to—the whitefaced men had so many powerful things, like guns, they must have powerful manitous as well. His sunbeamed head was moving slowly from side to side, like a man in a trance. Or maybe, it occurred to Meyokwaiwin, like a man whose eyes aren't wide enough to take in what's in front of him.

Maybe none of the whitefaced men had ever seen anything of the land on this side of the salt water except the woods country and the rocky barrens to the north. Maybe, for all their powerful things, none of the whitefaced men had ever had any idea of what might be beyond the woodlands. Until right now.

Meyokwaiwin looked past Kelsey to see what he was seeing. There was waist-high grass and higher, in every shade of green, stretching farther than any eye could see and rolling in waves as the breaths of summer breezes blew across them. But the green was just a background, like the base colour in a quillwork pattern. It was the time of year for the tall yellow flowers that blossomed in clusters of little buds and were good for making dye, or a tea for sore throats. So it was also the time of year for sunflowers, and for the smaller, many-petalled flowers that came in sky-blue, soft purple and milk white. There were white flowers with yellow hearts, yellow flowers with brown hearts, and there were pink and red and orange flowers and flowers of such an in-between mix their colours didn't really have a name. All of the colours were dancing and shifting with the wind.

Kelsey softly murmured something in words Meyokwaiwin didn't understand. She was standing nearby him, so she said, "Huh?"

"Oh." He looked back over his shoulder and seemed a bit embarrassed, though he couldn't hide that his eyes had stretched so big they threatened to break open his head. He said in her own language what she guessed he must've just said in his: "A sea of flowers." She smiled and looked out at the prairie again and nodded that he was right.

Kelsey told Meyokwaiwin's father they should get the line moving again, and seemed a bit apologetic for causing the stop. Morning Wolf explained to Misstopashish that on the prairie they wouldn't travel in a single-file line. The grass would spring back up from one person's footsteps, but many footsteps following the same line would leave a trail. So Morning Wolf, Kelsey and Clawface took the lead, walking side-by-side a ways apart, and the rest fanned out behind them.

They walked toward the setting sun until it touched the horizon, with no sign of an end or any island of trees in Kelsey's "sea of flowers." It was a dry camp that night, except for the birch bark water bottles they'd filled at the last stream before the edge of the woods. Meyokwaiwin and the other girls and women found a stand of the tall sunflowers that had much smaller heads than most kinds but also had juicy orange root swellings that went well with the dry sticks of smoked caribou meat in everyone's pouches.

In the night, Meyokwaiwin was awakened by a rustling sound. She opened her eyes and looked around. It was Kelsey, standing up from his bed and moving away from the camp. She sat up and watched him. He didn't go far, just a few steps and then turned around in slow circles, sometimes with his head leaned back and sometimes not. She was quite sure he couldn't see her sitting up, but she could see his standing shape against the stars. Out on the prairie, the night sky was like a bowl of stars sitting upside down on the plate of the earth. She understood why his head wasn't always leaned back: looking straight ahead he would still see starry sky. Something about a boy who was almost a man but still so full of wonder made her smile.

Partway through the next morning, Meyokwaiwin saw that the far edge of the sky was growing dark. Most of the others were taller than her, so they'd probably seen it already.

On the grasslands the far edge was a long way away, but the storm clouds looked to be moving fast. Soon she could see a haze of rain looking soft from a distance but must be a hard rain for her to see it that far off. A splinter of white light shot down from the black cloud, and a few steps later came a roar of thunder that cracked the sky. Thunder on the prairie was a very different thing than in the forest. As the echoes of the crash faded away, she felt a drum thumping under her left breast.

Meyokwaiwin's father held up his arm to halt. They all gathered towards him. He said, "If the lightning hasn't tired itself out by the time it gets here, then it would not be a good thing for us to be the tallest things on this plain. And if the storm keeps moving so fast, then the rain will come down on us hard, but not long, before it moves on. So I think the best thing for us to do is hunker down and cover ourselves."

Clawface grunted, "And pray there isn't hail." Everyone laughed, because there was nothing else they could do. Everyone except Misstopashish. Maybe whiteface men had a different sense of humour, or maybe he didn't understand what a hailstorm could do on the open plains. Meyokwaiwin had once seen a wide stretch of tall grass prairie smashed and flattened by hailstones as big around as the circle of her thumb and forefinger. But she'd only seen it when the hailstones were already melting on the ground, after she'd crawled out from under the skirts of a low evergreen in the island of trees where she and her family had taken shelter. Likely she never would've seen what that storm had done, or anything else ever again, if her father hadn't said: "*If there's hail in those clouds, then we're safer getting in under those trees and hope they don't draw lightning.*"

But this time there were no sheltering trees within the whole vast circle of the horizon, and anyway this storm seemed to have a lot of lightning in it. Lightning tended to shoot at the tallest trees around, and on the prairie that meant any tree at all. Meyokwaiwin crouched down, took the caribou hide out of the top of her packbasket and draped it over as much of herself and the basket as it would cover. She watched Kelsey unroll the strange, grey, unblanketlike blanket from around his bedroll, then take the ramrod out of his gun and plant it upright in the ground. He squatted down behind the ramrod, pulled the grey cloth up behind him and over his head, hooked its front edge over the ramrod, and just like that he was sitting in a little tent. When the rain hit, she was amazed to see the pelting raindrops spatter or bounce off when they hit Kelsey's tent. A well-smoked hide, like the one draped over her, wouldn't stiffen up when it got wet but still soaked water in as much as any hide that wasn't living.

Morning Wolf's "if this then that" proved right again as usual. Soon the storm was past and they were walking toward the sunset again. That night they ate the last of the smoked caribou. In the morning there was nothing to put in their mouths but the last few drops from the water bottles, and nothing that could be done but start walking again. No kind rabbit or prairie grouse offered to show itself, although many birdsongs proved there was life hidden in the grass all around. Very well hidden. But Meyokwaiwin told her ears and her stomach that if prairie birds were anything like woodland birds, then the ones she could hear the most would be barely a mouthful anyway and there were a lot of mouths in the carrying party. Usually the birds with the biggest and sweetest songs were the tiniest and greyest.

And that was, after all, a good arrangement, Meyokwaiwin told her stomach and ears. Because if those birds were as big and bright-coloured as their songs, they'd be easy hunting and good eating, so there wouldn't be many songs left to hear. Her ears agreed with her; her stomach didn't.

The sun was halfway up its hill when Meyokwaiwin began to see a distant, wavy line of green above the sea of flowers. Trees meant water. A little farther on, she could see a grey thread waving up from the green. Smoke meant people. Unless it was the terrifying curtain of a prairie fire, and this wasn't.

When they got near enough to the line of trees to see them as individual trees, Morning Wolf held up his hand to halt. Then he nodded at Kelsey, and the two of them walked on alone. Meyokwaiwin heard sharp clicking sounds all around her, and looked from side to side. It was the men who had guns doing the thing they had to do to make them ready to shoot—like nocking an arrow.

Meyokwaiwin's father stopped a little ways in front of the woods and began to speak in a loud voice. Someone who didn't know better might think he was talking to the trees. Morning Wolf was the only man of Misstopashish's helpers who could speak the buffalo people's language. It actually wasn't all that different from Meyokwaiwin's people's, it just took a little getting used to. But Meyokwaiwin had heard that there were other buffalo people farther west whose language was as different from hers as Kelsey's was.

In not very long, a wide line of men with bows and spears stepped out of the woods. In the middle of the line was a grey-haired man who wasn't holding a weapon, just a carved and painted staff he leaned on.

After Morning Wolf and Kelsey and the grey-haired man had talked awhile—or more like Kelsey and the grey-haired man had talked, and Meyokwaiwin's father had interpreted—Kelsey turned around and waved the others forward. It seemed that now that Morning Wolf had led the way to the buffalo people he was no longer the leader, just the inter-preter. And not long after they got settled into the buffalo people's camp, he wasn't even that.

The camp was down in the ravine made by the stream Meyokwaiwin's dusty mouth had been hoping for. The leafy green light was a relief from the blaze of the prairie sun. Kelsey spread a blanket out in the middle of the camp and sat down on one end of it to give presents to the grey-haired man, whose name was Okenanisu—Seven Stars. Each pres-ent—an axe head, or a knife blade, or a little bag filled with beads—naturally required a lot of talk. Meyokwaiwin could see Kelsey listening carefully to how her father interpreted his words, and what the differences were. He just as care-fully watched the hand-talk signs that helped out the words. After awhile, Kelsey was talking straight to Seven Stars, and Meyokwaiwin could see that her father wasn't happy about it.

Not that Kelsey didn't make mistakes and get words confused, making for laughter that he didn't seem to mind. Meyokwaiwin wondered if maybe that was the secret to how Kelsey could so quickly find his footing in a world that must be as strange to him as his would be to her. Maybe it wasn't a trick of whitefaced magic after all. Maybe it was just that he wasn't afraid to ask to have something explained to him, wasn't afraid to admit he didn't know.

Seven Stars apologized sadly that there wasn't enough food in the camp to make a proper feast for the visitors—in fact, the camp had been going pretty hungry for the last few days. Meyokwaiwin was quite sure that having no feast didn't make Seven Stars nearly as sad as it made her stomach. Her stomach had gone without food for longer than a day and a night before, but that didn't mean it wouldn't complain about it. "Soon though," Seven Stars said, "we may have plenty. One of my young men just came back off the plains, and said he saw three buffalo by a waterhole the storm had filled. We were just now, when you came, talking of the best way to sneak close enough to kill one."

Kelsey said, "No need to sneak close," and patted the long-shooting gun lying beside him. Seven Stars glanced down, then up again as though he'd seen nothing unusual. He hadn't reached the age of grey hair and wrinkled skin by showing all his thoughts on his face, but Meyokwaiwin guessed he'd never seen a gun of any kind before.

Meyokwaiwin wandered away from the palaverers, back down to the stream the camp was built around and scooped up a few more mouthfuls of cool, fresh water. Then she wandered through the camp, looking around but trying to not be too rudely curious. It seemed a big camp to her; she counted fourteen tents. But she knew it was a small camp for the grasslands people, who travelled in much bigger bands than the woodland people. There were dogs everywhere, running and barking or lying in the shade. The buffalo people didn't use canoes; they travelled on foot and used their dogs to carry things. Meyokwaiwin had seen the buffalo people on the move, their dogs wearing funny-looking arrangements of two long poles with the short ends crossed over the dog's neck, and the long ends weighed down with a pack back behind the dog's tail. When they got to where they were going, the poles became tent frames. They covered their tents with sewn-together buffalo skins, not birch bark or woven mats. All in all, it seemed a strange way to live, but Meyokwaiwin suspected her ways would seem strange to them.

While Meyokwaiwin had been being careful to not seem too rudely curious, it hadn't occurred to her that she might be a curiosity. She realized the children were staring at her. She furled the right side of her hair further forward, ducked her head sideways and went back to the centre of the camp, where at least the people she'd travelled here with were used to the way she looked. They weren't there, or at least none of the men were. Neither was Seven Stars and many of the men of the camp.

They came back some while later, with their lips and chins streaked with blood from eating fresh buffalo liver. Meyokwaiwin had eaten buffalo liver once, and her mouth wet itself remembering the taste and texture. But she had two sensible reasons not to begrudge the men wolfing it all instead of bringing even a little back to camp. One was that they'd done the hunting, after all. The other reason was that buffalo liver was nowhere near as delicious if it wasn't eaten right then and there, sliced steaming out of the fresh kill, so any brought back to camp wouldn't've been the same anyway.

Kelsey had killed one buffalo. All the other men with guns firing at the same time from the same distance had managed to hit another one. Kelsey seemed happier about having finally seen a buffalo than about finally having something to eat, but then he'd already had something to eat—his first taste of buffalo liver. Seven Stars told him grandly that there were much bigger buffalo that travelled in immensely bigger herds farther out on the plains. He said that Kelsey should come with him to see them when the camp moved west. Meyokwaiwin saw her father and Clawface glance at each other, and their eyes were hooded and guarded.

A few men had stayed with the dead buffaloes to stand guard. Meyokwaiwin went with the other girls and women to do the cutting up and carrying back. With so many hands it didn't take long.

It was a wonderful feast of buffalo meat roasted sizzling on spits, buffalo meat wrapped in wet clay and baked on a bed of coals, buffalo meat boiled into a thick soup... Sage from the prairie and juniper berries from the ravine made the baked and boiled parts even tastier. They all ate under the stars around the big council fire. Children ran in and out of the circle, laughing and eating at the same time; women sang cooking songs.

Kelsey sat beside Seven Stars, and Meyokwaiwin happened to be nearby when Seven Stars said to him, "The buffalo you killed—I will have my wives make the wooly part of his hide into a proper buffalo robe for you. And paint it with pictures that will be big medicine for you."

"Thank you."

"But it will take some while to do. The hide must be pegged out and stretched and scraped, then tanned and worked-over to make it soft, then smoked, then..." Seven Stars shrugged his age-twisted shoulders. "We must leave this place soon to go join up with other bands, and find a big herd to get meat for the winter. If you come with us, by the time of the Frost Exploding Trees Moon my women will have made you a buffalo robe to keep you warm."

"I thank you, but I already have a wintering place prepared, back along the way I came. There are many things cached there waiting for me. But when the winter ends, I will come back this way again. Since I won't be starting from near so far away as this year, I should be back in this place sometime around midsummer."

"If you're sure you will be back, I will have a buffalo robe waiting for you."

"I give you my promise I'll come back, and bring guns to trade for beaver pelts."

"You promise?"

"If I live."

Seven Stars shrugged his shoulders again. "If we all live."

Something about what Seven Stars and Kelsey had been saying to each other made Meyokwaiwin glance around to see if her father or Clawface were close enough to have overheard. They both were.

A few days later the camp broke up and went its separate ways: three separate ways. The group that had come with Kelsey started back toward the sunrise. The buffalo people packed up their fourteen tents and headed toward the sunset, but not all together. Because they'd have to rely on what they could find to eat along their line of travel west, it was better to split into two smaller groups travelling quite a ways apart, so they'd have twice as much prairie to forage from. Eight tents went with Seven Stars to head a bit north before turning west. The remaining six tents set off south, and would eventually turn west, too.

Meyokwaiwin was surprised to see how much the prairie had changed in just a few days. It was now a sea of green and autumn gold, as the pink and purple flowers faded and fell and the last flowers to bloom were all shades of yellow.

The night after leaving the ravine to head back eastward to the woodlands, Meyokwaiwin was wakened by a rustling sound, just as she had been on their first night on the prairie on their way west. This time it wasn't Kelsey. It was several men, all larger than the little giant, and all trying to move quietly. She recognized the movements of her father in one of the vague shapes silhouetted against the stars. All of the men snuck away in the same direction, into the tall grass and away from the camp.

Meyokwaiwin didn't know why she should feel afraid, but she did. Something told her she had to know what her father and the other men were doing. She thought of crawling along after them, keeping low to the ground. But dragging her body through the grass would make a lot more sound than footsteps. She stood up, bent forward so her head was lower than the tops of the grass and flowers, and followed in the direction they'd gone.

Now she had definite good reason to be afraid. No matter what her father and the other men had snuck away from camp to do, they wouldn't be happy if they caught her spying on them. She moved slowly, and every few steps pushed her hands out in front of her, palms together, then spread her arms to part the grass so it wouldn't hiss against her hunched-over body. She almost laughed, picturing that anyone who caught sight of her would think she was trying to swim through the grass. Even if she hadn't choked it back, it would've come out as a nervous laugh; there would be nothing funny about the men she was following catching sight of her. She began to hear low voices up ahead. She took a couple of more careful steps till she was close enough to hear words in the voices, then crouched down and strained her ears.

Her father was saying, "In years past, when I have traded for an iron knife and such, the man I bought them from had brought them from a ways east, where he'd bought them—probably from you."

"Probably," said Clawface.

"I know that man paid you fewer beaver and fox pelts for that iron knife than he would sell it to me for. And you paid much less when you bought it from the white men at the salt water than what you sold it for. But that is just the natural way of trade."

Clawface and the other canoe men muttered noises of agreement, and of appreciation that Morning Wolf understood they weren't thieves, just traders.

"But now," Morning Wolf went on, "Misstopashish has come all the way here. If he goes back and tells the other whitefaced men they too can travel here, even out onto the plains, and get more furs for their knives and blankets than they would at the salt water, why should they not? You would not be traders anymore—you would just be paddlers and carriers."

There were murmurs of unhappy surprise from the canoe men. Once again, Morning Wolf's manitou had shown him an "if this then that" which others hadn't seen. But Meyokwaiwin didn't hear Clawface's growly voice among the murmurs. She guessed that Clawface wasn't surprised because he and her father had already been talking about this between themselves.

From out of nowhere, Meyokwaiwin felt a tickle at the back of her nose and knew she was going to sneeze. She clamped her hand over her mouth and nostrils to hold it in. The sneeze turned into just a tiny explosion behind her nose, which hurt a little. Much worse than the hurt was that it made a tiny grunting sound.

The men's voices stopped. Then one of them hissed, "What was that?"

Meyokwaiwin stayed crouched like a fear-frozen rabbit and tried not to breathe.

Meyokwaiwin's father said, "I do not come out onto the prairie often enough to know the sounds of all its creatures. But I can tell you that whatever that was it was not a wolf or a bear, so we have no need to tremble." There was low laughter from the others, then Morning Wolf went back to what he'd been saying, "And then there is the problem of the buffalo people. We trade with the buffalo people, yes, but that does not mean they are our friends. Even you whose home country is farther east must've experienced their raiding parties."

There were mutterings from the other men, some angry and some sorrowful.

"We can rarely raid *them*," Meyokwaiwin's father went on, "because they live and travel in much bigger bands than us. And that is also why it's so much easier for them to organize big raiding parties, because their chiefs have much more power over them."

One of the canoe men grunted disgustedly, "That's no way to live."

Morning Wolf said, or his manitou said through him, "We can't change the way we live, nor that it makes us weaker than them in war. But, now we have guns. And in not many more years we will have traded for many more guns. The buffalo people do not have guns. Things are going to change."

There were many happy murmurings at that, and Meyokwaiwin guessed it would've been happy shoutings if the men weren't trying to keep their voices from being heard in the camp.

"Or things *would* change," Morning Wolf's voice dashed water on their fire, "if not for Misstopashish. You heard him tell the buffalo people he would come back next year with guns to trade. And if the next year he goes back to the salt water and tells his people of his travels, the *next* year there will surely be many more whitefaced men coming to trade guns to the people of the plains. So, if Misstopashish safely finishes this journey..."

There was a silence. Meyokwaiwin had seen her father do that before, say, "*If this, then what?*" and let everyone else stew in that a while.

After a moment, one of the canoe men said flatly, "Just knock him on the head and leave him for the wolves and crows."

"No!" Clawface's voice came out much louder than they'd been speaking up till now. He lowered it immediately. "The whitefaced men have manitous of their own. The men in the fort at the salt water have ways of knowing things. I have to go back there in the spring to trade, and if we have killed their friend and stolen his goods, they will know."

There was another silence, then Meyokwaiwin's father said, "So then what should we do?"

No one spoke a quick answer, and Meyokwaiwin held her breath so she wouldn't be heard while the only other sound was the soft sighs of the night breezes breathing on the sea of flowers. Finally Clawface said, in a tone that suggested he'd been waiting for someone else to say it, "Misstopashish saved your child from two bears."

"My *girl* child," Meyokwaiwin's father said as though correcting him. "And the one least likely to give me grandsons, unless she meets up with a blind man." There was some laughter at that, held down and kept low. "So Misstopashish killed two bears and got himself a name, so what? That is but a small thing beside the big things we council on tonight. What I have said to you tonight remains the same, none of you have disputed it, and the question is still the same. What should we do?"

V

KELSEY WAS AWAKENED by fierce sunlight blazing through his eyelids. He sat up, blinking. Something was wrong, or at least very strange. The sun was halfway up the sky. It shouldn't be. Usually he was awakened by the sounds of everyone else breaking camp and packing up to get on the move again, and that was usually at the first glimmers of dawn. Especially since the days were getting so much shorter and daylight travelling time wasn't something to be wasted.

Kelsey sat up and looked around. The tramped down circle of the camp was surrounded by a wall of tall grass and flower stalks, too high for him to see over on his knees. There was no one inside the circle except him. There were some things, though: his rifle and the other things he carried, and the beaver pelts that Seven Stars had given him as presents in courtesy for all the things that Kelsey had given him. His birch bark water bottle was still there where he'd left it last night, but he could see no others. All of the packbaskets and other carrying devices were gone; the only shoulder pouches left were the two he carried.

For a moment, Kelsey thought he must've been sleeping too soundly to come awake when the rest of the camp did, so they'd finally got fed up and gone on ahead, leaving him to catch up. But in the centre of the circle was a neat stack of blankets topped with a few axe heads, knife blades and bags of beads. Those were the things he meant to give the carriers when they all got safely back to their riverside camp and his expedition's canoes. A quick glance told him they hadn't left behind any of the things he'd already given them along the trail, so were already officially theirs. It seemed as though they'd meant to steal away and leave him there, but wanted him to know they hadn't stolen anything.

But why? He hadn't had any arguments with any of them; it seemed to him that he and they'd been getting along just fine. Maybe he'd gone and broken some kind of taboo without knowing. Or maybe they hadn't gone far and he was getting himself worked up over nothing.

Kelsey slowly and warily got up onto his feet, but didn't stand straight up. He kept his back bent—something told him not to raise his head any higher than he needed to see over the wall surrounding him. When he did, there was nothing to see but the surface of the sea of flowers fading into the distance until it blended with the base of the sky. He crouched down again, picked up his rifle and cocked it, then stood up straight and slowly turned around in a circle, squinting and peering hard.

Even looking from his full height, such as it was, there was nothing to see in any direction except the endless waves of grass and flowers. Kelsey shouted, "Hallo!" then, "Wachiye!" There wasn't even an echo; the wind just took his voice and carried it away. It occurred to him that if he kept on shouting he was just as likely to draw the attention of people or creatures whose attention he didn't want.

He sat back down to try and think. But the more he tried to think what to do, the faster his heart raced and the harder it was to breathe; as though that huge and uncaring sky was sucking the air out of his lungs. He thought of following the trail of the ones who'd left him behind. But there would be no trail—that was the whole point of walking across the grasslands in a wide line instead of single file. He thought of trying to find his way back to the ravine where Seven Stars had offered to take him west for the winter. But even if he could find the ravine, there would be no one there now.

Kelsey tried to take hold of himself and focus on small practicalities. He opened one of his shoulder pouches and counted the strips of smoked buffalo meat Seven Stars had given him, then shook his water bottle against his ear. He had enough food for maybe four days' travelling, and water for three, if he rationed himself. The question was: travel where? There was no point travelling west, but if he could travel far enough east get to the western edge of the woodlands, there would be plenty of little streams to drink from and refill his water bottle. But he had no way of knowing which way was east or west, on this flat land with no landmarks to judge from.

There *were* ways to find out, like planting his ramrod upright in the middle of the tramped-down circle and laying stones or little flower heads at the tip of its shadow as the morning sun moved it west, or the afternoon sun east. But that would take some time. Then it occurred to him that he could find his directions in no time from the bed he was sitting on. He'd got into the habit of laying out his bed so that his head was toward the path ahead and his feet toward the path they'd come down. So, that end of the bed with his still rolled-up coat for a pillow was pointing east, at least roughly. Even with no landmarks to take a bearing on, he could keep himself walking generally eastward by keeping his shadow generally on his lefthand side, since the sun was already pretty far to the south at this time of year in these latitudes.

Feeling much better now that he had a plan, Kelsey turned around to turn his bed into a bedroll, as he had a hundred times since leaving York Factory. The doubled canvas he used as a groundsheet was actually four times as wide as his bed, so as he had all those other mornings he double folded its double fold around the blankets, rolled it all up and tied it, then sat down on his bedroll to look around at what to pack up next.

His eyes lit on the stack of beaver pelts, and then the stack of trade blankets with the axe heads, knives, and bags of beads on top. There was no way he could carry all of that, or even half. It would not impress the Governor at York Factory if "the boy Kelsey" came back with no accounting for a good portion of the goods he'd been entrusted with. But now that that came to mind, how did this Kelsey boy hope to get back to York Factory at all? Or even to the wintering place he'd set up halfway back along his route?

Even if he could manage to make his way across the prairie to the western edge of the woodlands, he had no way of knowing whether he'd be north or south of the mouth of the path Morning Wolf had led the way on. And even if he found the mouth of the path, it wasn't exactly a well marked or well beaten path, and there'd been a lot of twists and turns on the way from the camp by the river. And what exactly did he plan to eat while he was blundering around in the forest, after his dried buffalo meat ran out? It was one thing to bring down a buffalo or caribou with his rifle once the Indians had found them for him, but that wasn't hunting, it was just shooting. And he had no idea of which plants were poisonous and which the human stomach could take. Looking around at the circle of tall grass and wildflowers surrounding him, he couldn't even tell which sunflowers were the kind that had nutritious orange tubers in their roots. Without Indians to help him, the Little Giant was just a boy lost in the wilderness. As the hopelessness of Kelsey's situation sank into him, and every "maybe I could–" ran into a dead end, it seemed the hedge wall around the camp circle started whirling, closing in like a noose...

"Kelsey!"

The voice wasn't quite a shout, just pitched to carry a bit of a distance. It hadn't come from above, and Kelsey didn't believe in guardian angels anyway, or any kind of angels. He took hold of his rifle, stood up and turned in the direction the voice had come from.

What he saw was the most beautiful thing he'd ever seen in his life: the girl Meyokwaiwin wading toward him through the sea of flowers. Maybe there were angels after all.

Kelsey propped his rifle in the crook of his arm so he could wipe the heels of both hands up across his wet cheeks and eyes, pretending to be just pushing his hair back. As Meyokwaiwin gradually got closer, he had time to realize that she was coming from the direction he'd decided was west. That didn't make sense, not if the Indians had meant to leave him behind and continue on their way east.

As Meyokwaiwin stepped out onto the flattened camp circle, Kelsey said—trying to keep his voice from shaking—"What, um, what's happened?"

"This is not when to talk. I will tell you as we go. We must get moving."

"Moving where?"

"Back to the camp where your canoes are."

"But..." Kelsey gestured at the two piles of beaver pelts and trade goods. "I can't leave all these things here, to rot or get stolen. My, uh…" He realized that explaining "masters" to an Indian would take a long time. "I will be in big trouble if I do."

"You think you're not in trouble now?"

"I could bury them, but that could take a while, and I don't even have a…" He tried to think of an Indian word for shovel. "…digging stick."

"My packbasket is almost empty, but it won't hold all this. We could cache the rest up in a tree where no one would see."

Kelsey just angled his head from side to side as though looking around, thinking it should be unnecessary to point out there was nothing resembling a tree within the whole, vast circle of horizon. Meyokwaiwin just crouched down, shrugged off her back-basket and started filling it from the pile of blankets and trade goods. She said, "Your blanket-that's-not-a-blanket, that you put under your bed—"

"The canvas."

"Your can-vass is big enough to make a bag to put all the rest of these things in. We tie it to your gun and make your gun a carrying-pole between us. When we get to the forest, we find a good tree and hang the bag up in it. It'll be safe a long time, the can-vass holds out rain, I saw. But we must hurry."

Kelsey didn't argue. In not very long they were walking east—the same direction Kelsey's bed had told him was east—with Meyokwaiwin in the lead and the rifle now a shoulder-pole between them. As they walked, she told him of the conversation she'd eavesdropped on last night, and the conclusion that her father and the other men had reached. "If they did not knock you on the head, just snuck away quiet and left you there, then they could truly tell the other white-faced men they had no idea what happened to you. And if we only carried away the things you had already given us, then it could truly be said we did not steal anything from you. And if when we passed by back this way again in a few days, and if a scout sneaking ahead found you were gone but left all the things you could not carry, then those things would just be found, not stolen."

"But...why would you be 'passing back this way?' That is, why did you go west, I mean all of you, instead of keeping on east for home?"

"The men wanted to catch up with the buffalo people. Not the bigger bunch that went with Seven Stars. The smaller bunch of six tents. Once we got a little ways away from you, all of the men with guns ran on ahead, told the rest of us to wait for them in the ravine. A little ways later, I told the others I was feeling stomach-sick and would follow after them. Then I snuck back here."

"But...why did the men with guns want to catch up with the buffalo people?"

"To kill them."

Kelsey stopped dead. Meyokwaiwin was almost pulled off her feet, but managed to stay upright without letting go of her end of the rifle. Kelsey was too stunned to apologize. He sputtered, "*Kill* them? Why?"

"Because they are not us. Next summer, some of them might come to raid and kill some of us, if we did not kill them first. The women would make more children to grow into warriors, if we did not kill them. We do not take slaves."

"But that's...crazy."

"Is it? Is it crazy that two grizzly bears will try to kill each other? Is it crazy that a pack of wolves will kill a stranger wolf in their territory? Do your people never have wars?"

Kelsey was going to say that civilized wars were entirely different. Then he remembered that the year after he arrived at York Factory, a group of raiders from New France had appeared out of nowhere at Moose Factory and The Company's other two posts south of York, and the Frenchmen hadn't been dropping by for tea. Kelsey liked to think the English would never carry on so uncivilized as the French, but he wasn't so sure. So he said nothing. Meyokwaiwin said she wanted to shift the weighed-down rifle to their other shoulders before they started walking again. So they did, and then they did.

They walked until there was just enough light left to set down their burdens, draw the rifle barrel out of the corner-knotted canvas bundle and roll out their beds. Kelsey found the ground a bit colder, and the squashed-down grass stalks a bit pricklier, without the canvas under his blankets, but it did seem foolish to unknot it and dump everything out only to have to turn it back into a bag in the morning. He also found the night sounds more than a bit stranger. All the other nights since he'd left York Factory, whether camped in the woods or on the plains, the sounds of the wild had been buffered by the sounds of a dozen or more other human beings around him, snoring or snuffling or murmuring in their sleep. Now there was only Meyokwaiwin in her bed a few feet away from him, and she didn't snore much. The hissing of tall grass in the night winds might be creatures out hunting, and the hooting of night birds and distant wolf howls definitely were.

Kelsey was tired enough to sleep through most of the night anyway, despite too many unfamiliar sounds in the air and no familiar canvas between him and the ground. Partway through the next morning, Meyokwaiwin said over her left shoulder—she almost never turned her face back over her right shoulder—"What is this can-vass stuff?"

"Oh, it's, um," Kelsey fumbled in vain for an Indian word close to "sailcloth." "It was made for, um...the big canoes that my people use to travel on the salt water. They're far too big to paddle, so we hang big pieces of canvas above them, and the wind, um—"

"*Yukastimon*," she tossed back at him without breaking stride. "Mostly no good for rivers, but on big lakes when the wind is right we stand a pole up in the canoe, with a thin-scraped hide or tight-weaved grass mat, and the wind pushes us along."

"Oh. Just the same." Kelsey wondered which part of him had assumed that these ignorant savages hadn't put together the basic facts of wind and water. If his little expedition had travelled across a few large lakes, instead of always on winding rivers or tree-hemmed little lakes that weren't much more than a swelling in the river, he probably would've seen Clawface and his crewmen hoisting sails. Kelsey reminded himself for not the first time that there were a lot of different brands of ignorance.

It also occurred to him that crossing a few large, horizon-stretching lakes might've prepared him a little for the prairie sky. Logic told him that the prairie sky wasn't any bigger than the ocean sky, but when he'd crossed the ocean the ship had always been slanted upward or downward with the hills and valleys of waves all around, and there'd always been the sails, masts and rigging overhead. Here there was nothing overhead or all around except the sky, giving the feeling that everything else was just little bits of nothing, including human beings.

Kelsey and Meyokwaiwin sometimes jogged along to cover more ground than just walking. But only for short stints, because the improvised carrying pole was awkward and Kelsey wasn't sure how much good all that bouncing was doing for his rifle barrel. After they'd slowed down from one of those jogging stints, Kelsey had time to notice that even some of the newer, yellow clusters of flowers were starting to fade and lose their tiny petals. Probably had something to do with the patches of frost that'd been on his top blanket that morning. Old Man Winter wasn't on the doorstep yet, but the flowers could already feel his breath.

As if she'd heard what he was thinking, Meyokwaiwin said, "Where is the place you plan to spend the winter?"

"Oh, well I can tell you how far it is, more or less, by adding up the numbers on my papers, and more or less the sort of direction. But just...sort of more or less."

"But you said the marks you made on the paper would tell any whitefaced man where you'd travelled. And 'any' would mean you, too, wouldn't it?"

"Well, um, sort of." Kelsey was starting to feel helpless again. "The marks I made each day could tell you how far I travelled that day, or my best guess, and whether we had to carry the canoes and all from one stream to another. But when it comes to finding one particular..."—he couldn't think of an Indian way to say "needle in a haystack"—"...place in all these woods and rocks and rivers..." He trailed off.

"What is the place you look for?"

"Well, I gave it a name, but it wouldn't mean anything to anybody. It's a neck of land that pokes out into a river, a river almost wide enough to be a lake, and there's a lot of tall pine trees there..." That didn't sound like he was narrowing it down much. "Well, when we first left the salt water to follow the sun, there was a lot more canoes than just the three that came to your camp. But when we got to the place I need to get back to, most went off in different directions. Clawface

76

told me that next spring everyone who wants to go to the salt water to trade will meet there again, and travel together for safety."

"Oh." Although Kelsey could only see the back of Meyokwaiwin's head, he could see it nodding. "The Going-North Place. I was there once with my family, though we didn't go north."

"Do you know how to find that place again?"

That seemed to catch Meyokwaiwin so much by surprise that she looked back over her right shoulder, showing the sloped side of her face. She quickly turned her head forward again, but the expression Kelsey'd seen in that instant was as if he'd asked her if water flowed downhill. She said, loudly enough for him to hear with her back to him, "I told you I was there once."

"Could you ... would you ... guide me there?"

"What else is there for me to do?"

The flat and forlorn way she'd said that brought home to Kelsey the enormity of what she'd already done. He'd noticed that Indian families weren't very strict about children being obedient, but Meyokwaiwin had gone against her father's wishes in a very drastic way. Betrayed, some might say. She hadn't said she was afraid what Morning Wolf and Clawface might do if they caught up with her and Misstopashish, but she definitely wanted to travel as far as possible between each sunrise and sunset, shaking him awake the instant dawn started to break. It might well be that she had cut herself off from her own life to save his.

Once they were back in the woodlands and dappled shadows, Meyokwaiwin seemed to ease up a little. Now they could even have a campfire, partly because building a safe fire in the rocky woodlands took less time than on the grasslands, partly because the smoke and light wouldn't show for miles as it would on the prairie. Meyokwaiwin gathered some nuts from under a brown-leafed tree and they roasted them in the coals. But even now they didn't talk much: it was eat, sleep, wake up and start moving again.

The rifle carrying-pole and canvas-wrapped bundle were a lot more awkward in the woods, but they didn't have to struggle with it long. Meyokwaiwin stopped on the path and pointed with her free arm and said, "There!"

Kelsey said, "Where? What?"

"Just the tree we need."

Kelsey followed her point to a thick, tallish pine tree—not so tall as to have an impossibly long stretch of bare trunk before the boughs started. They set down the canvas-wrapped bundle, Kelsey freed his rifle from it and Meyokwaiwin knelt down to take off her back-basket. When she stood up again, she looked from the tree to the canvas to her packbasket and said a little sadly, "We're gonna need a rope." She untied the ends of her tump line from the basket and held it up in both hands, looking down at the dark red flower design on the wide forehead piece. She said, "There is a crumbly reddish rock you find in some places. You have to grind it and grind it and grind it to make it powder. Then you have to take the shells off many sunflower seeds and grind the seeds to make an oil, and you very carefully heat up the oil without it catching fire, and then you can mix in the red powder—not too much, just enough. Then you can start to paint." Meyokwaiwin looked around and shrugged. "Oh well, I don't see any other rope around here."

Kelsey said, "We can take some of the things out of your back-basket—so's it won't drag too heavy on just your shoulder straps—and squeeze them into the canvas. Just keep what you'll need on the way back to the river camp. I left plenty of things there, you can take what you want."

Once that was done, and one end of the tump line tied to the retied canvas bundle, Kelsey shinnied up the tree trunk with the other end of the tump line clamped in his teeth. He got himself perched on the first bough, about twice his height from the ground, took hold of the tump line with both hands and looked down. Meyokwaiwin crouched, with her knees on either side of the bundle, wrapped her arms around it as far as they would go and heaved herself to her feet as he pulled on the line. She boosted the bottom of the bulging bag as far as she could, and once it got too high for her hands to help him he felt like the weight would pull his shoulders out of their sockets. But he managed to get it up balanced on the branch and wedged against the tree trunk. It would have to go a ways higher, though, to have enough thick-needled boughs around it to stay safely hidden.

Kelsey took the end of the tump line in his teeth again and wormed and squirmed his way up the corkscrew ladder of pine boughs. He told himself he should be happy he was in one of those rare situations where there was actually an advantage to being smallish. But he had to keep blinking his eyes to keep bits of pine needles from falling into them, and his hands and hair grew sticky with pine gum. When he guessed he'd got high enough he looked down again, wondering if he had the strength to pull the bundle up by himself. It turned out he didn't have to. Meyokwaiwin was perched on the bough beside it. He thought it must've been rough on her bare legs shinnying up the tree trunk.

Once they'd got the tree cache safely tied in a pine nest and got safely back to the ground, they laughed at the whiskers of pine needles stuck to each other's faces. Meyokwaiwin plucked a few off his cheeks to show him. But when Kelsey reached out to do the same on the flat-sloped right side of her face, she flinched and turned away. She said, "We better get going again."

They travelled a lot faster without the heavy bundle slung between them, even though the woods path had a lot more ups and downs than the prairie, and was laced with tree roots that could twist an ankle. Meyokwaiwin seemed to have eyes in the toes of her moccasins, while he was watching the ground in front of every step. Kelsey suspected she was holding herself back to the best pace that he could manage. But on their third day in the woods she slowed down and seemed nervous. Kelsey wondered if maybe she didn't have any more idea than he did of what to expect when they got to the river camp and had to explain why they'd come back alone.

At one point Meyokwaiwin said over her shoulder, as though it was something she'd been thinking about for awhile, "The canoes you came in—every one of them is too big for the two of us to manage."

"They aren't mine anyway. They belong to Clawface and his people."

"My family has three canoes, and one of them is small enough for two people to paddle. A few of the axe heads or knives you left at our camp will pay for it, and we can't carry all the things you left there anyway."

A while farther along the path that Kelsey wouldn't've known was a path—not without Meyokwaiwin to lead the way—he caught a whiff of woodsmoke. He began to hear the murmur of a river under the rustling of the trees, and then children laughing. When he and Meyokwaiwin stepped out into the clearing around the camp, it was the children who spotted them first, and came running. The adults followed at a more dignified pace.

Meyokwaiwin told them, "We had to hurry on ahead of the others because Misstopashish has to get back to the place he means to winter at and I can guide him there."

Kelsey wasn't familiar enough with Meyokwaiwin's mother and uncle to read their expressions, but he thought he saw a trace of suspicion. But Meyokwaiwin quickly moved the conversation on to what would be a fair price for the small canoe and two paddles, and a repair kit of birchbark and spruce gum in case of accidents along the way. They settled on one axe head, two knives and a small bag of assorted beads. Which was even more than Kelsey would've expected to pay for a canoe at York Factory, where iron goods weren't nearly as scarce and canoes didn't grow on trees. But as Meyokwaiwin had said, the two of them couldn't carry all his things anyway.

Meyokwaiwin had things of her own to gather together, so as she was doing that Kelsey ferried blankets and axe heads and such down to the canoe, guessing how much freight it could carry without swamping, and how much he and Meyokwaiwin could carry when they had to go around waterfalls, or from one stream to another. That still left a fair pile to leave behind, but that would stand as the promised payment to the guides and carriers who'd brought him to the sea of flowers. It struck him funny that only a couple of months ago he would've thought it ridiculous to leave presents for those who'd abandoned him to die. But, he'd got used to the fact that the Indians thought in a different way than he did. Not that he understood it completely, just understood it was different.

He was settling the last few things into the mid-part of the canoe when loud and angry voices broke out in the camp behind him. For an instant he was afraid that Morning Wolf and Clawface and the others had caught up with him and Meyokwaiwin. But that didn't seem likely, given the head start he and Meyokwaiwin'd had and how hard she'd pushed them to cover as much ground as possible every day. And anyway, the voices were female. Kelsey picked up his rifle and went toward the sounds.

Meyokwaiwin and her mother were tugging at either end of what looked like a rolled-up fishnet, although the threads looked coarser and thicker than the ones Kelsey'd had to mend for The Company. Meyokwaiwin's mother was screaming, "You can't have our fishing net!"

Meyokwaiwin screamed back, "Who gathered all the stinging nettles and boiled them to take the sting out and then rolled them back and forth on her bare legs to make them into cords? And who spent many winter nights knotting the cords into a net? Not you, not anybody else, just me! It's mine!"

Kelsey found it a bit odd they were both going so wild over a hank of fishnet; Meyokwaiwin seemed to've slid back into a tantrumy child. But then, she hadn't asked any questions when he'd said they had to haul all those trade goods along with them and find a place to hide them. So instead of saying, *"Who cares about a piece of old fishnet? Leave it,"* he cocked his rifle. It wasn't a particularly loud sound, but sharp mechanical sounds weren't common in an Indian camp. Everybody looked at him. Meyokwaiwin's mother let go of her end of the fishnet. Meyokwaiwin scooped up her back-basket and some pouches and brushed past Kelsey, saying, "Hurry."

They quickly got into the canoe and pushed off. Kelsey had automatically climbed into the bow, since the stern was where the steering happened and he guessed she knew more about paddling canoes than he did. He heard snuffling sounds behind him and realized the reason she'd wanted to hurry into the canoe and away was she'd been about to start crying. He decided to not look back until the sounds stopped. When they did, he said over his shoulder, "I haven't... thanked you proper-like for, um, doing what you did—coming back to get me."

"You rescued me from being bear food, what else could I do?"

"Oh, um, well... thank you anyway."

It seemed to Kelsey that their canoe was skimming along more swiftly than the ones he'd come in, even though there were only two paddlers and one was inexperienced and one was a girl. Then he realized that of course now they were paddling with the current, not against it. Almost all the journey back to where he wanted to get to would be downstream. Which meant that those eleven days in his journal of the trip upstream would be more like seven or eight travelling downstream. Depending on whether Meyokwaiwin actually did remember how to get there.

It seemed she did. Hers was a different kind of memory than Kelsey was used to, seeming to pop out in bits and pieces from the landscape. She would suddenly say, "Oh! Around this next bend you'll see a big pink rock on your left. From there there's a path over a hill to another river. It'll probably take us till nightfall to carry the canoe and all across, going back and forth." And when they rounded that bend, there would be the rock and there would be something vaguely like a path, and by sunset Kelsey and Meyokwaiwin would be laying out their blankets on either side of a campfire on the shore of a river flowing in the direction they wanted to go.

All of their campsites were the same bone-weary routine: cook, eat, collapse into a dead sleep until sunrise. Meyokwaiwin provided most of the food. In the mornings she would hang a fishline with a float and baited hook off the stern of the canoe, and in the evenings set her fishnet in the river. A netful of breakfast without wasting travelling time showed Kelsey that the tug of war with her mother hadn't been just a tantrum. While Kelsey was building the evening's campfire, Meyokwaiwin would explore the nearby woods and usually find at least a few mushrooms and edible greens. Once, she spotted a pair of little black ducks paddling up ahead of their canoe, and became quite excited at the prospect of duck dinner. Kelsey sadly had to explain to her that the one disadvantage to a gun with a rifled barrel was that it couldn't be loaded with birdshot like a smooth-bore. And even if he managed to hit so small a target, the large ball his rifle fired wouldn't leave much duck to cook.

All in all, Kelsey was feeling pretty much useless, until one late afternoon when they were looking ahead for a clear spot along the riverbank to camp and saw instead a lone caribou come down to have a drink. They stopped paddling and drifted with the current as Kelsey slowly raised his rifle and took aim. The caribou raised its sweeping-antlered head as though it heard something, and Kelsey's shot took it just behind the shoulder. Meyokwaiwin shouted, "Hai! Misstopashish!" and Kelsey felt less useless.

They decided that that would be as good a place to camp as any. As soon as they'd beached the canoe, Meyokwaiwin went straight to the dead caribou and knelt beside it. She put her hand on its forehead, between the antlers, and said, "Thank you, little sister, for giving us your life." Then she went back to the canoe for her skinning knife.

They had a grand feast of roast caribou spitted on Kelsey's rifle ramrod and turned slowly over the fire—a larger fire than usual, to scare off any forest creature that might be drawn by the smell of fresh meat and caribou blood. It wasn't elegant dining, they just sliced pieces off the outside of the roast as the cooking worked its way in, but Kelsey was sure even the Officers' Mess at York Factory wasn't serving anything half so good tonight. Meyokwaiwin said the rest of the meat wouldn't spoil for a few days. "And by then we'll be at the place you want to go, and there I can build a slow fire to smoke-dry what we haven't eaten."

True to her word, two days later the river widened and took a sharp turn to the left, and there was what Kelsey had been looking for: a tall white cross standing at the tip of a point of land. Meyokwaiwin said from the stern, "What is that?"

"Oh, it'll be easier for me to explain once we get up to it."

They found a low spot on the bank to beach the canoe, then picked their way up moss-slick juts of black granite to the sandy spot where the cross stood. Now Meyokwaiwin would be able to see for herself that it was made of two lengths of birch trunk with the bark still on, and a mound of stones anchoring its base. She said, "It looks like what we use to hold a sail over a canoe, but much bigger. Did you plan to sail this piece of land away?"

Kelsey started to laugh, and then realized that was exactly what the cross was meant to've done, taken that piece of land away. But it wasn't a very big piece of land, and the Indians didn't seem to object to having a trading post here and there. He patted the shaft of the cross and said, "This is a sign, a totem. A sign to other white men, if any come this way, that this land..." He decided not to say "has already been claimed." "A sign that another white man was here first. I..." "Christened" wasn't a word he was likely to find in any Indian language, so he settled on, "*named* this place Deering's Point."

"What is a Deering?"

"Sir Edward Deering is a man who lives in the country I came from."

"A friend of yours?"

"No, I couldn't say that." Well, they'd been in the same room once, but it was a very big room with a lot of other people in it.

Meyokwaiwin seemed confused. She said, "If he is not a friend of yours, why would you name a place after him?"

"He is a very important and powerful man." To say the least. Sir Edward Deering was on the board of governors of the Hudson's Bay Company, along with various other knights and lords and princes. There was a pretty good chance that when Sir Edward Deering learned that a young servant of The Company had named a place in North America in his honour, a place farther inland than any white man had gone before, he would remember the name Henry Kelsey whenever it came up in a report. But that was a lot to explain to Meyokwaiwin, or any Indian, so Kelsey just said, "He is a chief of the tribe I belong to now. Anything I do that pleases him will be good for me."

Now Meyokwaiwin seemed more than confused, she seemed surprised and shocked. She said, "So you are...a slave?"

Kelsey opened his mouth to correct her, then closed it again and lowered his head. Looked at from Meyokwaiwin's world, that was exactly what he was: a slave.

VI

MEYOKWAIWIN DIDN'T KNOW what to think when Kelsey dropped his head and turned away from her. She didn't know if maybe she'd insulted him by calling him a slave when he wasn't, or if maybe he was but it was a secret he hadn't wanted anyone to know. He raised his head again, but didn't turn toward or look at her, just said over his shoulder, "I should show you the real reason I wanted to get back here before winter," and started walking farther onto Deering's Point. She decided he probably wanted her to follow him.

Although the tip of Deering's Point was just windswept sandgrass, as it widened out there were a few scraggly pine trees and then the same thick spruce woods as along the rest of the riverbank. A tribe of black-scalped, buckskin coloured chickadees—*kichekanases*—flittered and twittered among the spruce twigs, paying no attention to the two earthbound creatures lumbering by. Meyokwaiwin began to see something white through the trees up ahead, something like a snow-covered hill but long before the first snowfall.

They came out into a clearing and there was something like a birchbark wigwam, but different from any wigwam Meyokwaiwin had ever seen. Not all wigwams were round-roofed, some had pointed tops like this one and like the tipis of the buffalo people. But the pointed ones were still round at the bottom. This one had a wide, flat triangle for a front, with a straight line at the bottom and slanted walls running straight back from either side of the triangle and joined at the top. The straight-sloped side walls, with no roundness to them, put Meyokwaiwin in mind of the flat right side of her face.

The strange-shaped thing also looked bigger than any wigwam Meyokwaiwin had ever seen—not all that much taller or wider than the biggest she'd seen, but because it wasn't round it could be as long as it wanted, and this one wanted to be long.

Kelsey moved a couple of slabs of birchbark from in front of a squared-off doorhole, saying, "I'll have to build a better door before winter," then stepped inside and beckoned her to follow him. The only light inside came from the doorway, and from a square hole in the roof that Meyokwaiwin guessed must be for a smokehole. It took a moment for her eyes to get used to the closed-in dusk. The place was empty, and she had a feeling that if she said anything it would echo. Kelsey was already walking ahead, almost bouncing on his feet. The downcast spirit that had taken over him a few moments ago was definitely gone. She followed him.

Halfway down the slant-walled cavern was a stone fire circle with old ashes in it. Nearby was a pile of deadfall firewood and brush. Kelsey knelt by one end of the pile, pushed some of the firewood aside and scraped at the earth with the back of his knife. He reached his fingers down into the loosened earth and pried up the end of a pole that fit in his fist. He kept pulling and prying and pushing, and out from under the pile and the earth beneath it came something that looked something like a spear—except that the spearhead was much bigger than it should be, was made of iron and was rounded-in and didn't have much of a point on it.

Kelsey stepped over to the circle of stones and ashes and said, grinning, "Do you notice anything strange about the fire circle and the smokehole?"

Meyokwaiwin looked up, then down, then both again. She said, "It's not straight above, it's..." she moved her hand down on an angle.

"That's right. But anybody who stumbled across this place, even if they did notice about the smokehole, would just think the people who built this place were a bit," and he tapped the side of his head and made a silly face. "We only made one fire here, just a twig-fire to make some ashes. As soon as this place was built, we were back in the canoes and heading west. Here, help me move some of these," and he picked up two of the fire circle rocks.

She helped, but it was very confusing. If he wanted the fire circle moved to the right place, why hadn't he put it there in the first place? But it seemed he didn't want to set the rocks in a new circle yet, just move them away from the old circle. And they'd only moved half of them when he said, "That's enough," and quickly picked up his odd-looking spear. He was doing everything quickly, and seemed as excited as a boy with his first toy bow and arrows.

Meyokwaiwin sat down to watch and see what the boy was up to. He drove the point of his wide-headed spear down into the ashes, then put one foot on its flat top and pushed down. When he stepped back and pried with the handle, up came a big scoopful of earth with the ashes, like the strange thing was more like a spoon than a spear. Meyokwaiwin saw now that it was a kind of digging stick, but one that could do a lot more a lot quicker than any digging stick she'd ever seen.

She watched Kelsey dig up the whole ash bed one spearhead-layer deep, piling the earth outside the half circle of stones, and then step down into the wide, shallow hole and start to dig some more. Then her eyes began to drift away, around the inside of the wigwam that wasn't a wigwam.

With the tawny orange side of the birchbark facing inward, the place did have a warm look to it. But she wondered just how warm it would actually be when the winter winds started hitting those long, flat walls. She could see that all along the bottom of both side walls, before their slant reached the ground, there was a double line of staked logs stacked on top of each other. Meyokwaiwin nodded to herself that that would help keep warm air in and ground creatures out. Looking upward and around, she could see that the strange wigwam was made in a way she could understand, and should hold up to the weather. Halfway up both the slanted walls was a sideways pole that a skeleton of slanted poles leaned against on their way up to a roof pole at the top of the triangle. Sheets of birch bark had been layered across the skeleton to make the wigwam's skin, and Meyokwaiwin had already seen that on the outside there were more poles slanted up the walls to hold the birch bark down. All of that was well and good, and basically the same way wigwams had always been made, even if this one was a funny shape. But still, she had to wonder how warm any place this big was going to be without three or four or five families living in it.

Meyokwaiwin realised the digging sounds had stopped. Kelsey was leaning on the handle of his digger, breathing like he should maybe sit down for awhile. The problem with getting excited was you sometimes tried to do more and faster than you should. She said, "Would you like me to dig for awhile?"

He grinned at her like he wouldn't mind and said, "Well, if you really want to try out the shovel..."

She tried out the word a couple of times as she went to take hold of the thing itself. As Kelsey let go of the handle he said, "When we get down about this far," and held up one forearm with the hand straight, "we'll have to start being careful."

That didn't seem like all that deep to dig, except that the circle Kelsey had dug out was wider than she was tall. She went to work trying to imitate what Kelsey had been doing, except at a more sensible pace—stab down, bend back and lift. After awhile it began to feel natural, and it was fun to see she could move so much earth by herself.

After a while more Kelsey said, as though he'd heard what she'd been thinking about this big empty wigwam and the winter cold, "Clawface and a couple of his paddlers were going to bring their families here to spend the winter. But now I guess it's going to be just the two of us—that is, if you're going to stay."

"Where else do I have to go?"

Kelsey didn't seem to have anything to say to that, just got up and took another turn at the shovel.

Once they'd dug down about as far as Kelsey'd said, he began to poke the shovel down gently without standing on it, and scrape it along something underneath. What was underneath looked to be a sheet of canvas, except when Meyokwaiwin helped him brush away the last few pellets of earth it had a more oily feel than the canvas bag they'd hung in the tree.

Kelsey furled the covering back and began to lift things out. After not very long he'd taken so many things out he had to climb in to get at the rest, and still there were more things. Meyokwaiwin could only sit on the edge of the hole and gape. There was a big iron pot like her mother wanted, another one even bigger, and two smaller ones, all filled with bags of other things. There were knife blades and axe heads of all kinds of sizes, and other iron things she couldn't guess what were for. There were blankets layered in between things or wrapped around them, as though blankets were such a common article they could be used just for padding. There was a small wooden box that Kelsey looked at confusedly, as though he couldn't remember what was in it. He shook it against his ear, then smiled and opened the lid and held it up to her.

Meyokwaiwin looked in and saw what looked to be little metal circles, some not so little, all joined together like a chain. She started to reach in, but Kelsey said, "Careful!" so she pulled her hand back and just peered closer. She saw that the things inside weren't joined together but jumbled together. They were metal fish hooks, with sharper barbs and surely less likely to break than the ones her father carved out of bone.

Kelsey set the box aside and went back to lifting things out of the pit. Among other things there were two black-brown bundles of long leaves all wrapped together. Meyokwaiwin's nose told her it was tobacco—not kinnikinnik but real tobacco from far away—but she'd never seen so much of it in one place, or such big leaves.

After a few more things, Kelsey lifted out a canvas-wrapped bundle as long as he was tall. A grin almost too big for his face blossomed as he set it down. By now there were so many things piled around the rim of the pit he only had room to set it down lengthwise away from him, so had to stretch his arm out hard to unwrap the canvas but kept on grinning. Inside the canvas were two guns, not as long as Kelsey's rifle but more like the same kind he'd traded to Morning Wolf. Kelsey said through his grin, "Tomorrow we shall have roast duck." Meyokwaiwin wasn't so sure about that, so just nodded.

The last two things to come out of the pit were two of the stumpy wooden things that Meyokwaiwin now knew were called *kegs*. Kelsey climbed out after them, heaved one of them up with both hands and carried it over to a back corner of the long wigwam. He set it down there carefully and came back saying, "We'll leave that one there and not let any fire come anywhere near it, not even a spark. That one's filled with gunpowder.

"And this one..." Kelsey picked up his hand axe and cracked the head of the other keg. He pried out a piece of wood just wide enough to get his fingers through, then came out with a strange, yellowy-white, squared-off something that he held up between his thumb and first finger. It was longer than wide, wasn't very thick and had some little holes dotted through it in lines. Meyokwaiwin looked from it to him, wondering if she was supposed to know what it was. He winked at her and stretched one corner of his mouth out of shape to fit one corner of the thing in between his back teeth. He bit down hard, there was a crunching sound and the yellowy-white thing came away from his mouth not quite square anymore.

Kelsey didn't swallow or chew, just held the thing out to her, saying thickly around the piece still on his tongue, "You have to hold it in your mouth and wet it a bit." Meyokwaiwin imitated what he'd done, but when she crunched down she wasn't sure whether it was the thing or her teeth that were breaking. The piece of it on her tongue felt like powdery stone. She worked the corners of her mouth to squeeze more moisture into her mouth. When the piece-of-thing got soft enough to chew, it tasted a little like the baked cakes made from cattail roots, but not much, more salty and more ... something else.

After they'd both swallowed, Kelsey said, "It's much better when you got some soup or something to dip it in. It won't ever rot, so long as you keep it dry. So it's useful for the men who have to spend many days on the big canoes sailing across the salt water. It's called hard-um..." He'd said *musko*, which meant "hard" but wasn't really a word by itself. It got put into words to mean "hard-something"—like *muskowask*, "hardwood," or *muskowetahao*, "hardhearted." But he couldn't seem to think of a way to say the something that went in the name of this hard-to-bite stuff, so he just put the nibbled piece back on top of the keg and got up to rebuild the fire circle.

Meyokwaiwin helped him move the stones to straight under the smoke hole. Then she emptied the birch bark rogan she'd thrown some of her things into back at her family's camp, and carried it down to the river to get water. The sun was already touching the treetops on the other side of the river, though the day hadn't been very long yet. They were well into The Moon When The Geese Fly, so if Kelsey truly believed they were going to have a roast duck dinner it would have to be soon.

For her first time ever cooking with an iron pot Meyokwaiwin didn't want to use the hugest one, but it did seem a handy thing for storing water in, being as how the river wasn't just outside their door. So she kept going back and forth trying to fill the big pot up with her one birch-bark bucket, telling herself she would make another rogan as soon as they got settled in. As she came and went, she saw in stages that Kelsey had started a fire and was building it up in between rummaging through his piles of treasures, as though there were some things he wanted to bring close to the fire before it was the only light left.

When the huge pot was about three-quarters full, Meyokwaiwin decided that was enough and instead poured her latest trip's water into one of the smaller pots. She put some chunks of caribou in, and then wondered how she was supposed to put the pot onto the fire to cook without smothering the fire. Kelsey reached behind him and came up with three iron bars that he set across the fire with their ends resting on top of the fire circle stones. Once the pot was sitting on the bars, Meyokwaiwin had to remind herself that she didn't have to worry if the flames licked up around it, or even if Kelsey tossed some twigs on beside it to flare up more light. He was fussing with some things on his side of the fire circle, but she couldn't see exactly what.

The hard-somethings did get softer soaked in caribou broth, and the two tastes were good for each other. But when Kelsey said the hard-things would stay good eating for a very long time in the keg, if it was kept plugged from mice and worms, she said they should be saved for eating only when there was nothing else to eat. The moon that followed the Frost Exploding Trees Moon wasn't called the Starvation Moon for nothing. That was the moon when the terrible Wendigo roamed the icy woods and would take possession of people so crazy with hunger he could make them eat their own children.

When the pot was empty, Kelsey moved the bars closer together and put a different pot on them. It was a very different pot, much smaller than any of the others but with much thicker walls and bottom. It had a handle coming out of one side, and a little pinch-out on the rim that Meyokwaiwin guessed was for pouring. Kelsey reached down beside him and came up with a strange grey rock that just fit in the palm of his hand and, from the way he held it, was heavier than its size. It was shaped something like an overturned canoe, flat on the bottom and rounded on top. Kelsey said across the fire circle, "I have some bigger ones, but we don't want to be at this all night," and plunked the stone nose-down into the pot. He built up the fire some more, and sat waiting.

After not very long, Meyokwaiwin could hear a hissing sound, and a sharp strange smell needled the inside of her nose. She leaned up and forward so she could see inside the little pot, and then fell back with a squawk. *The stone was melting!*

Kelsey bugged out his eyes, waggled his fingers beside his head and said something that sounded like *oo-ga boo-ga*. She could feel herself starting to get angry or embarrassed or both, but then he shrugged. "Finding mushrooms that aren't poison is magic to me. But I need you to help me with this magic. That pot you made the soup in, I need it filled with cold water, about..." He held his hand sideways with the fingers together. "...that far from the top."

Meyokwaiwin took the soup pot over to the huge pot and dipped it in, glad that she'd thought ahead about water. When she lugged the pot back to the fire circle, the tail end of the grey stone had disappeared into the little pot and Kelsey was fiddling with another strange black iron thing. It had square corners—the whitefaced men seemed to like squared-off things—and was shaped kind of like the book thing Kelsey made marks in, except it had a wood-sheathed iron handle sticking out of one side. Kelsey motioned her to kneel and pointed the handle at her. "You have to hold it straight, all right?"

"Yes." She wrapped both hands around the handle tight to keep them from going shaky as he lifted the pot off the fire and poured smoking rock juice into two holes on the top of the squared-off thing. After awhile of careful pouring he put the pot back on the fire and slid his hand between her hands around the handle, the palm of her right hand against the smooth back of his, and the back of her left hand feeling his rough-callused palm. She slipped her hands away as he took hold. Then he swivelled to lower the squared-off thing into the pot of water but kept hold of the handle. The pot hissed and steamed.

Meyokwaiwin leaned forward to look. Kelsey put both hands on the handle and the whole thing opened up like a leaf that'd been folded down the mid-vein. Through the steam, Meyokwaiwin saw something like two stiff strings of shiny grey beads dropping into the water. Kelsey said, "That's likely all I'll need for tomorrow, but as long as we've got the, um..." He seemed to grope for a word in her language, but couldn't find one so used one in his. "...the *lead* melted, we might's well finish it off."

They filled the "mould"—as Kelsey called it—two more times, dunking it in the pot and opening it again. Then Kelsey dabbled his fingers in the water to test the heat, reached in and came out with seven or eight tiny lead balls held together with a short lead thread between each. He said, "*This* is roast duck."

"Yes, and I'm a purple butterfly."

Kelsey began to cut the lead beads free and drop them into a pouch beside him, so Meyokwaiwin pulled another string out of the hot water and did the same. By the time they were done, she could feel her head getting too heavy for her neck. It had been a very long day with a lot of new things

97

in it. She unrolled her bed on one side of the fire circle, and could hear Kelsey doing the same on his side. That was the last thing she heard until the morning birds.

In the morning Meyokwaiwin went into the woods to cut some live boughs to make a drying rack to smoke cure the rest of the caribou meat. When she came back into the clearing with an armload of sticks, Kelsey was coming out of the "house"—as he called it—carrying all three guns. He set down his rifle and one of the shorter guns, propping them against the front of the house, and came toward her carrying the third one. "I'm going to try my luck out on the river, paddle a ways upstream and then drift down, maybe surprise a duck or a goose. I don't *think* anything big enough to hurt you will come out of the woods while I'm gone, but just in case, I'll leave you this one and show you how to use it."

He showed her how to pull the hammer back, which wasn't an easy pull. Then she imitated what she'd seen him and other men do—lifted the gun up to her right shoulder and pressed her cheek against the wooden part so she could peer one-eyed along the barrel. She thought if he made a joke about the flattened-in side of her face being perfect for fitting against the flat part of the gun, she would shoot *him*. The gun didn't seem to want to balance in her hands; it kept trying to fall forward and down. Kelsey stepped behind her and put his arms around her arms and his hands on the backs of hers. As he moved her left hand forward and her right hand a little downward, she got a warm and dizzy feeling from him being so close and holding her. Meyokwaiwin told herself not to be stupid. She was just a clumsy girl with a squashed-in face, and he was just showing her how to hold a gun.

He stepped away from her and pointed at a wide-trunked tree with falling leaves, about twenty steps away. She pointed the gun at the tree trunk and pulled the trigger. The back of the gun punched hard against her shoulder, as he'd warned her it would, and the smoke and sparks stung her eyes. She lowered the gun, blinking, and said, "Did I hit it?"

"No, but I think it moved." He took the gun from her and reloaded it. "Just wait till something gets in close before you fire, and aim for the widest part. If it's a wandering hunter thinking of turning thief, he'll likely know what a gun is and back off as soon as you point it at him." He handed her the loaded gun, then said as though the answer mattered to him, "You'll be all right?"

"Yes. Will you?"

"Oh, um..." The question seemed to surprise him, or maybe the way she'd said it. "I can't get lost staying on the same river. I don't think."

Once Kelsey was gone, Meyokwaiwin sat down and wove together a loose framework out of green twigs. As her fingers worked, her mind and her heart wandered into an emptiness. Every other time she'd smoke-dried meat or fish, it had been with her mother and other women and girls, and there'd been singing and chatter and laughter. She tried opening her ears more to the singing of the forest birds and chatter of the squirrels, and that helped a little. Maybe she could get used to thinking of those sounds as the voices of her family and friends. But soon most of the birds would be gone and the squirrels denned up for the winter.

Once the drying rack was woven together, Meyokwaiwin found a rocky spot to build a small fire she could safely leave alone, then went looking for something to make a hood over the drying rack to hold the smoke in. Back behind the house there was a big pile of sheets of birch bark. It seemed that in building such a strange-shaped wigwam, like no one had ever built before, Kelsey's canoe men had cut and peeled and flattened a lot more bark than they'd ended up needing.

Meyokwaiwin carried a small sheet back and half-hooped it over the drying rack perched on four forked sticks above the fire. As she cut the caribou meat into strips and tended the fire, she kept looking at that big wigwam with the flat sides that the winter winds would hit hard with only two people's warmth inside it, and thinking of the pile of birch bark sitting behind it. The pile was a lot bigger than she and Kelsey could've gathered together, even if they'd had days and days to do it—what with carefully cutting and peeling, gently malleting any black spots so they wouldn't stick to the tree and tear, then stretching each sheet out flat on the ground weighed down with stones, and each sheet separate so the damp rising out of the ground would help take the coil out of it. And anyway, even if some miracle stretched out autumn long enough to get all that done, birch bark was best gathered in the spring or early summer, when the fresh-running sap made the trees' skin loose around the trunk. But there was all that birchbark already gathered and flattened out, just sitting there...

After some while, Meyokwaiwin heard a sound that might've been a dry twig snapping nearby, but she knew it was Kelsey's gun much farther away. Some while later, Kelsey came up from the river carrying his guns and a fat redheaded duck. While they were plucking its feathers off, and Kelsey was showing her how to find and cut out the little pellets so there wouldn't be roast lead in their duck dinner, Meyokwaiwin said, "That house is gonna be cold come winter, with just the two of us in it, the way it is."

"You think so?"

"I know so."

"Well, I don't think we can invite your family to come stay with us."

She squinted sharply at him through suddenly-misted eyes. If that was meant to be a joke, it wasn't a very good one. She shook it off and went on, "There's a lot of already-cut birch bark lying around back of the house, and a lot of moss and fallen leaves lying all around here, and this time of year the cattail heads down by the river are getting all puffy and fluffy. We can put that new birch bark across the poles holding the old bark down, and fill the space between with moss and leaves and cattail fluff. That'll keep the cold out better."

"I guess it would."

"Only problem is, we'll need a lot more poles to hold down the new bark."

"Oh, that won't be much of a problem with a steel axe and saw. When we were putting up the house we didn't cut down *every* young poplar on Deering's Point."

So they went at it, over days and days, putting on the lowest row of birch bark first so the layer above would overlap and rain or snow would flow down instead of in. Kelsey cut poles while Meyokwaiwin gathered moss and leaves and cattail heads, piling it on a sheet of canvas and then folding the corners up to drag it back to camp. As they worked together on their winter home, Kelsey fell into the habit of calling her Meyo for short. Meyo, like musko, wasn't really a word but a part of words: *meyomakwun* meant "a nice smell," *meyototamitoowin*, "a good friend." But Meyokwaiwin didn't mind, and it took away that sour reminder of "a pretty face." After awhile she started thinking of herself as Meyo.

They were partway through the second sidewall when a voice called from the river side of the clearing. Kelsey picked up his rifle, Meyo the gun he kept loaded with birdshot, and they went around the corner of the house to have a look. There were two men standing on the edge of the clearing, both holding a bow in one hand and an arrow in the other. Meyo didn't recognize either of them, but from the way they were dressed and the way they said their words as they and Kelsey spoke across the clearing, she knew they were of her own people. They and their families were on their way to their wintering grounds in the deep woods. This bend in the river was the carrying-place over to a smaller stream that would take them to where they always set their traplines.

Meyo murmured to Kelsey, "They're safe," so he un-cocked his rifle and told them they and their families were welcome to stay overnight. It took a while for the two men and their wives and children to get all their belongings and three canoes off the river, through the riverside woods and into the clearing. Meyo helped. She got the impression that their plan for today had been to get everything into the clearing, camp there overnight and carry everything over to the other stream the next day. So the only change in their plan was that they would have a roof over their heads tonight.

It seemed to Meyo that the women and older girls were getting an impression of her, too, and a wrong one. From sidelong looks and giggles, she guessed they thought she was Kelsey's wife. She knew that that could never be, but it was too complicated to explain the truth of how she and the white-skinned man-boy had come to be sharing the same wigwam.

There was more than enough room in the house for all the travellers to lay out their beds. But first there was a feast. One of the men had killed a goose on the river that morning, probably the last one of this year, and the women had pouches full of dried berries. They cut up the goose and Meyo put the pieces and some berries into one of the iron pots with a little bit of water. Kelsey brought out a few squares of his hardtack to dip in the gravy, which brought amazed grins onto chewing mouths. While the eating was going on, Meyo noticed the eyes of the visitors sliding across the fire circle to where Kelsey's treasures were piled on a sheet of canvas to keep the damp from rising into them. The two men's eyes kept fixing onto the guns.

When the eating was done, the bargaining was begun. One of the men went to the jumble of packs and baskets stacked just inside the doorway and came back with a buffalo robe. It wasn't a new buffalo robe, but that wasn't a bad thing. Buffalo robes got softer as they got older, and the wooly hair didn't wear off or wear thin. Kelsey got up and got a knife blade and a small axe head, and set them down in front of the buffalo robe. The other man shook his head and pointed at one of the guns. Kelsey shook his head and laughed. Fortunately it wasn't an insulting kind of laugh, just amazement that anyone could think a gun could be had for one buffalo robe. Even so, if Kelsey had been a little older—not still a boy who could be expected to laugh at odd moments—the two men from the canoes might've taken offense. And that would not have been good for anybody.

The bargaining went on in the roundabout way Meyo had seen and heard a hundred times. Maybe one of the men would ask Kelsey if he thought it was going to be a long winter, and Kelsey would ask what they thought, and they would talk awhile about how thick-furred the wooly caterpillars had been this fall and how early the ducks had flown south. Then one of the men would get up and go back toward the doorway and come back with maybe a quillworked pouch filled with dried berries, or a third of a moose hide that had already been put through the long process of turning it into rawhide that could be useful for a thousand things. The man would put down whatever it was on top of the buffalo robe and point at the gun. Kelsey would shake his head and put down maybe a large axe head beside the small one in front of him. And then one of the men would slide into a long story about the time he found an eagle's nest, or the time his brother fell through the ice...

As the two men grew more frustrated with Kelsey's head-shaking, Meyo began to get a little worried. The families who'd come in the canoes included two full-grown men and several almost-men, and all that stood between them and the gun they wanted—for that matter, all of Kelsey's guns and goods—were Kelsey and her. At another time of year the men would've had plenty to offer in trade for the gun, but it was the wrong season for furs. One of the men even went so far as to promise Kelsey that if he gave them the gun now, they would come back in the spring with many winter-thick pelts of fox and sable and beaver. Luckily Kelsey had the sense to not say he didn't trust their promise, just that no one could say for certain what might happen to anybody over the winter.

The younger children had already lain down to sleep, and now the older children and the women were starting to do that, too. Meyo's stomachful of warm goose, and the fact she wasn't going to put her voice into the bargaining anyway, decided her to do the same. As she settled into her bed, she glimpsed the eyes of one of the women flicking confusedly from Meyo's side of the fire circle to Kelsey's, as if noticing for the first time that there were two beds in this wigwam, not one.

Meyo lay awake for awhile, listening. The men's voices didn't start sounding angrier, but sleepier. That was good.

In the morning, the men started up on Kelsey again. It seemed clear that the travellers wouldn't be travelling any farther today, so the women and children helped Meyo with the moss and leaves and birch bark. Meyo felt natural again, having families around her working and joking together, even if they weren't her family. But then one of the women said to her, "That whiteskin man, Misstopashish, he's not your man?"

Meyo felt herself blushing. "I'm not old enough for that."

"You're older than I was when I had my first man."

The blush grew warmer. "He was lost on the prairie and I guided him here. So since I was here already, I figured I might as well wait out the winter here. That's all there is to it."

"Oh, that's all there is to it, eh?"

Meyo wanted to grab the woman by the throat and scream at her, *Look at my face! That'll always be all there is to it!* Instead she just mumbled, "I have to get something from inside," and hurried away.

She didn't really need to get anything from the house, just needed to get away and calm down. So when she stepped inside she paused and looked around to see what she might pretend she had to get. The daylight through the doorway and the smoke hole showed her something she hadn't noticed before about the jumble of packs and baskets stacked against the front wall. One of the bundles tied together for carrying was eight or ten new-made snowshoes.

Meyo had been wondering and worrying about what she was going to do about snowshoes. A person without snowshoes in the winter might as well be without legs. Struggling through the snow instead of walking on top of it would wear you down quickly. Meyo knew how to make snowshoes, or at least she'd helped her mother and father do it often enough to probably be able to do it herself. But first Kelsey would have to get lucky enough to kill another caribou, or a moose, so she could wrap the fresh hide in mud for seven or eight days and then scrape off all the fat and hair. If some of the hair was stubborn, she would have to sprinkle the wet hide with wood ashes and wrap it up for another couple of days before scraping again. That would give her the rawhide she needed to web the snowshoes with, but to make the frames she would have to find the right kind of tree branch and then shave and whittle and steam the wood to bend it into shape. Then she would be able to begin the long and complicated business of weaving the webbing into the frames the right way. The chances of getting all that done before the ground was knee-deep in snow were not good. Fortunately, for the last while she'd been too busy putting a thicker skin on the wigwam to think about snowshoes, and too tired at the end of the day to lie awake long, but it had always been gnawing at the back of her mind.

Meyo went toward the fire circle, where Kelsey and the two men were passing a long-stemmed pipe back and forth and seemed to be thinking of what to say next. The pile of homemade things in front of the two men hadn't grown much since morning, and the little pile of foreign-made things in front of Kelsey still didn't include the gun they wanted. Meyo leaned past Kelsey to pick up the knife blade she'd fitted with a wooden handle, as though that was what she'd come looking for. As her mouth passed close by Kelsey's ear, she whispered, "Snowshoes." When she straightened back up again, he gave the tiniest little nod, not looking at her.

Meyo went back out to the wall-thickening party and, happily, the nosy woman had found something else to chatter about. After not very long there were loud voices from in front of the house and everybody went to look. Kelsey was out in the clearing with the two joyful men and their new gun. He showed them how to load it, and they each took a shot at a nearby tree. The deal for the gun included enough gunpowder to fill a birchbark bottle, and thirty of the lead stones the gun fired, the same size stones as fitted Kelsey's rifle. Kelsey said that nistomitunow—three tens—was as many stones as he could give while still leaving him enough for the winter. Meyo knew he could easily make more, he had plenty of lead and a mould that was smaller than the one that made the bird pellets but made bigger stones one at a time. But she didn't say anything.

The next morning the travellers went on their way, leaving behind the buffalo robe and other things they'd piled up to trade for the gun, along with two pairs of bearpaw snowshoes. Over the next while a few other small bands of travellers passed through on the way to their wintering grounds, and they all knew beforehand that a whitefaced man was wintering at Deering's Point—even though they didn't know that was what he called it. Kelsey seemed surprised and confused that word of him had got around so quickly, and to people coming from different directions. Meyo was surprised that he was surprised.

Kelsey did a bit of trading with the travellers, but only small trades now, and mostly for winter food: smoked fish, sunflower root fruit, dried rose hips and berries, cattail flour...Meyo was glad that he seemed to've taken her talk of the Starvation Moon to heart. The first skin of ice on the edges of the river meant there would be no more travellers. Anyone with any sense would've got to where they were planning to spend the winter by now.

Meyo surprised herself by not being disappointed there'd be no more visitors. She had plenty to do, like making Kelsey a pair of high-topped snowshoe moccasins and beading a flower pattern on the toe pieces. Once the snow was deep enough that even Kelsey could see a caribou trail, he would go off hunting on stormless days—after she'd shown him how to cut marks on trees that would guide him home even if a sudden snowfall covered up his snowshoe tracks. And after she'd shown him how to walk in snowshoes without getting cramps in his legs, dodging snowballs when she laughed at him tripping over his own shoes.

Kelsey's hunting didn't get lucky very often, but there were only the two of them to feed. And one good thing about winter was you didn't have to worry about meat going bad; you just sawed pieces off the frozen carcass and brought them inside to thaw and cook.

In the evenings she and Kelsey would sit and talk across the fire circle, while their hands were busy with easy-going things like sewing rawhide seams or sharpening axes. She could hear him growing more loose and comfortable in her language, like someone talking across a campfire, not a council fire. They talked about the strange world Kelsey had come from, and about the parts of her world that were still strange to him, and about all kinds of things she'd never imagined talking to anyone about. They laughed a lot and were amazed a lot and were sad together about things in the past that had made the other one sad.

There came an evening when Kelsey came around the fire circle and knelt down close to her. *Very* close to her. He slowly raised one hand toward her face and she jerked her head away and to the right, as she always did whenever she caught someone staring at or reaching to touch her freakish face. He lowered his hand and his eyes and said in a small voice, "I guess I must look funny to you—funny, strange, ugly...with my frog's belly white skin and snubby little nose and pale eyes and yellow hair."

Meyo shook her head vigorously and said, "No, you don't." She put her hand on his shoulder and looked straight at him, trying to pull his eyes into hers so he would believe what she was saying. "Maybe at first, but now you look just like you."

Kelsey had lost what little brown was in his summer face, it was now just pink and white, so a red blush flamed. His thin, pale pink lips went up at the corners. He said, "So you see me the same way I see you."

VII

IT WAS DEEP IN THE WINTER and Kelsey was deep in sleep when a deep voice from outside Deering's Point House called, "Misstopashish!"

Meyo, snuggled up against him in their cozy bed, quivered and whispered, "Who could it be?"

Kelsey mumbled with sleep-numb lips, "I don't know." He'd thought it might've been a voice in a dream calling him, but not if she'd heard it, too.

"Misstopashish!" came again.

The square of sky showing through the smokehole was a pinky grey, so it was barely dawn. Kelsey reached one arm out from under the blankets and buffalo robe and tossed a few sticks onto the embers of last night's fire. Then he reached down to tug on his breeches rolled up at his feet to keep them warm, and sat up to pull on the wool shirt he used for a pillow.

"Misstopashish!"

Kelsey stood out of bed, picked up his rifle and padded barefoot to the door. The floor between the fire circle and the doorway wasn't all that cold; Meyo had laid down a thick layer of spruce boughs and covered it with the big sheet of oilcloth that had lined the cache pit. The winter door was a piece of canvas backed by three blankets, with their bottoms curled around a log to keep the wind from lifting them. Kelsey rolled the log back with his foot, furled the curtain sideways and peered out.

Standing about ten paces from the doorway was a lone Indian on snowshoes, with a musket in the crook of his arm. Even with a lynx mask fur cowl covering the Indian's forehead and the sides of his face, Kelsey recognized him. Clawface. Kelsey cocked his rifle.

Clawface held up his right hand and said, "I come a long ways, Misstopashish, and not to do you any harm."

"Like you meant me no harm when you left me alone on the prairie?"

Clawface swivelled his musket to point it at the sky and fired it off. Kelsey considered the fact that even though Clawface's gun was now empty, he still had a hatchet and knife in his belt. But then he also considered that if Clawface meant to harm him, he could've just hidden in the woods with his musket and waited for Kelsey to step out the door. Then again, Clawface might not've come knowing or expecting there'd be smoke coming out of the strange-shaped wigwam he'd helped build last spring. Maybe Clawface hadn't known that Misstopashish made it back alive to Deering's Point, and he'd come hoping to dig up all the treasures he'd helped bury.

With all those considerations in mind, Kelsey uncocked his rifle and said, "Come in."

Clawface knelt by the doorway to take off his snowshoes, then stooped under the door curtain Kelsey was holding open for him. Meyo had built up the fire and put a small pot of water on. From the pleasant combination of smells, Kelsey could tell that she'd put in some rose hips to steep along with some leaves of the shrub that was known at York Factory as Indian tea. Clawface said to Meyo, "Your father will be glad to know you're still alive."

She said flatly, "Will he?" The flatness seemed to be working against a choke in her voice.

The three of them sat down around the fire circle. Kelsey took out the long-stemmed, carved soapstone pipe he'd got in trade, packed in a mixture of foreign tobacco and local kinnikinnik, puffed it alight and raised it in the four directions as he'd learned to do. Then he passed it to Clawface, who took a couple of puffs and waved the smoke around his face, then handed it back as Meyo scooped the tea into three tin cups.

They sat sipping and puffing and not saying anything. Kelsey found it extremely strange, sitting silently with one of the men who'd left him to die on the prairie. Finally Clawface said, "I have known since the Flying South Moon that you are here. But I had to wait until my family had enough meat to last them if I was gone on a long journey. It is a very long journey on snowshoes from my family's wintering place to this place."

Kelsey didn't know what to say to that, since Clawface still hadn't said anything about that little event in the fall. So Kelsey just sipped his tea and puffed the pipe.

Clawface turned toward Meyo and said, "You did the proper thing, sneaking back to help Misstopashish."

She just said, "I know," and made Kelsey proud of her. She, too, wasn't going to give Clawface an inch.

"Morning Wolf, your father," Clawface said after a moment, "was very sad when we got back to the ravine and found you not there with the other women, and when they told us you had lagged behind and said you would catch up with them but didn't. He thought some of the buffalo people must've caught you alone and killed you or taken you for a slave. Then, when we got back to the river camp and your mother told us what you had done, he was very angry.

"But then he thought about it and we talked about it. He remembered that he had said, on the night we decided to leave Misstopashish behind, 'If Misstopashish can find his way back to his wintering place and find food along the way, then he was meant to live; if he wanders lost till he starves to death, then that was meant to be.' We had taken our hands off what was to happen, and put it into the hands of the winds and the manitous. So after Morning Wolf had been angry for awhile, he said, 'If my daughter helped Misstopashish find his way and stay alive, then that was meant to be.'"

Kelsey was looking back and forth between Clawface and Meyo. If Clawface had been expecting some sort of happy relief that her father had forgiven her, he didn't get it. Kelsey figured he knew Meyo much better than Clawface and *he* couldn't read her expression, or lack of same.

Clawface turned to Kelsey and said, "And so it is, and so it will be. You have my promise that I will never again do anything that might harm you, or not help you."

"Seems to me you promised last summer, when we set out from this place, that you would guide me to the land of the buffalo people and bring me back safe to this place before the rivers froze."

Clawface said, "Take out your knife."

Kelsey wasn't quite sure what to make of that. What he'd just said to Clawface could be taken as a pretty bad insult. He drew his belt knife out of the beaded moosehide sheath Meyo had made for him, keeping his peripheral vision on Clawface to see if he made any move to jump up or draw his own knife.

Clawface was a lot bigger than him, and had probably been in a few knife fights before.

Clawface said, "Now put the point of your knife into the fire, into the hottest coals."

Kelsey did so. After not very long, the tip of his steel knife was glowing as red as the coals.

Clawface said, "Now take your knife back out and point it at me." Kelsey did. Clawface reached out his right hand, took hold of the searing knife tip between his thumb and forefinger and said very deliberately, "What I have said to you this day is true." Kelsey believed him.

Clawface let go of the knife tip, stood up and said, "Now I must just step outside and stick my hand in the snow for a little while."

Clawface stayed at Deering's Point a few days, and went out hunting with Kelsey when the weather was clear. He could read animal signs where Kelsey saw nothing, and could tell at a glance which parts of the woods grouse would like to winter in. Not that Kelsey and Meyo had been starving, even though Kelsey's hunting depended more on blind luck than woods craft. There was a hole in the river ice they kept clear for fresh water, and sometimes Kelsey or Meyo would sit by the hole jigging a short stick up and down, a stick with a length of fish line with a baited hook. And Meyo had set rabbit snares in the woods around the house.

When Clawface left, he said he'd be back at Deering's Point in the spring, "But then so will tens of tens of others, gathering to travel to *Kichewaskahikun*," which meant "The Huge House," the Indians' name for York Factory.

As soon as Clawface was gone, Meyo spat out an imitation, "*You did the proper thing, little girl.* Pfft. *Pikwu'ntow*—" which sort of meant "nonsense" but ruder, "All of them, with their:

'Anything that's happened was meant to happen, and anything that didn't happen wasn't meant to be.' Means nothing."

"Well ... there is a certain kind of sense to it. If they hadn't left me alone out on the prairie, to let the winds and the manitous decide my fate, you and I wouldn't be here ... together ... the way we are."

She grabbed a side strand of his hair and gave it a tug, shaking her head and saying, "I think, Misstopashish, you gone even crazier than they are." But she was smiling.

What she'd said did make him wonder, though: why had Clawface made a long winter's trek to Deering's Point just to say he didn't mind that Meyo'd rescued Kelsey from the fix Clawface had left him in last fall? Well ... if Clawface hadn't made that trek now, then the next time he and Kelsey met up again — whether at Deering's Point or York Factory or somewhere in the wilderness — they both would've had a lot of awkward questions hanging between them, and maybe in no circumstances to sit down and sort them out. But now Kelsey was sure they were all sorted out. Pretty sure.

Clawface's departure also meant Kelsey and Meyo were left alone again, which Kelsey didn't mind at all. He was quite sure that Sir Edward Deering in his mansion had never had as pleasant winter nights as this poor apprentice boy curled up beside the fire with Meyokwaiwin, listening to the wolves howling in the hills.

Sometimes he tried to imagine what kinds of pictures she built in her mind of the bizarre things he tried to describe to her, things like stone houses with more than one floor, and carriages with wheels, and horses. He'd had buffalo described to him many times at York Factory, but the picture he'd built from those descriptions had been so skewed that when he saw his first musk ox he'd thought it was a buffalo.

But at least she could build some kind of pictures, skewed or not, of most pieces of his world. There was one thing, though, that was so strange to her she couldn't seem to make any sense of it at all. There was no word for "time" in her language. There were words for the moons and the seasons, for day and night, and for three days ago or three days from now, but time as a thing in itself didn't exist. Whenever he tried to explain or describe it to her, she would wrinkle her forehead and listen hard, but eventually her eyes would goggle and her head would start to shake from side to side and she would raise her hands in helpless defeat. Kelsey eventually admitted defeat, too, and decided there was no way to translate the idea of time into the Indian way of thinking. At times he caught himself wondering if the Indian way of thinking didn't make more sense.

But time did pass. The nights grew shorter and the snow began to melt, very slowly but treacherously. Now when Kelsey went out hunting he had to be careful of sinkholes. What might look like an even plane of snow might hide a dip in the ground where an air pocket had grown larger as melting snow seeped into it. No sinkhole was deep enough to drown in, but plunging hip-deep into half frozen slush when you were a long, cold walk away from dry clothes and a fire was not a healthy idea. So Kelsey's snowshoeing, which had never been all that fast at the best of times, grew even slower as he warily tested suspicious spots before putting his weight down.

One day he came across what he was sure were fresh deer tracks. Deer generally didn't move around in the full light of day, but by the tail end of the winter they were desperate to find food. Kelsey scooped up a handful of snow and sifted it down to see that the breeze was coming from the direction this deer was going in, so wouldn't carry his scent to it. Then he started to follow the trail.

He kept his eyes trained ahead on the hoof tracks and the snow on either side, except when Sir or Lady Deer'd decided to spring over something; then Kelsey would stop and scan around for where the trail started up again. It was amazing how far a deer could jump, even from a standing start in deep snow. The deer tracks weren't the only signs of life Kelsey saw. The spattering of black dots flicking and bouncing across the white weren't spots on his eyes, the first warning signs of snow blindness, they were springtails—ice fleas. And the rusty flecks bobbing around the skirts of a spruce tree were the wingtips of wapanukoses, snowbirds. There were a number of different kinds of birds that stayed for the winter, but the white snowbirds and white owls that hunted them were the only ones that came and went with the snow.

After a while of following the deer's trail—time did seem to blend together in the woods—Kelsey heard the last thing he'd expected to hear out there, a voice shouting: "Kelsey!" He stopped and turned around. Meyo came running out of the stand of poplars he'd just picked his way through. Running on snowshoes wasn't an easy thing to do, and Kelsey wasn't about to try it now, so he stood waiting. The deer trail had led him on a circuitous route through the clearing he was standing in, but Meyo cut straight across toward him. She was halfway across when she disappeared with a shriek and an explosion of snow.

Kelsey hurried toward her as fast as he could without getting his snowshoes tangled. As the thrown-up cloud of snow settled, he saw she hadn't entirely disappeared but was up to her waist in snow and the sinkhole underneath it. Her snowshoes had got twisted, so it took a bit of squirming and pulling to get her out and on her feet again. Once she was, Kelsey said, "What is it? Why did you—?"

"Look at the sky!"

He did, for the first time since he started following the deer trail. The sky had grown darker, and ugly black clouds were moving impossibly in different directions. He didn't know exactly what it meant, but if he'd looked up and seen it earlier he would've headed straight for home.

Meyo said, "We have to get back, fast!"

"Yes, you go ahead and I'll try to keep up." Since they'd be following in his snowshoe tracks, and hers on top of them, there'd be no need to break trail—otherwise it wouldn't've been very gallant of him to tell her to go first. But walking behind her meant he could see that her skirt and blanketcloth leggings were soaked through, and the slush that wasn't dripping off was starting to freeze.

The breeze turned into a wind that began to howl and then roar, driving sheets of sleet in front of it. Sometimes the sleet pounded into Kelsey's back, sometimes pelted into his face. He slitted his eyes and kept them squinted half-shut, and was sure Meyo was doing the same. Through the roaring of the wind came the cracks of breaking tree branches. One large branch flew through the air across their path about ten feet in front of Meyo, just at the right height to've taken both their heads off if they'd been moving just a little faster.

Kelsey began to shout to Meyo things like "Ain't far to go now!" and "We'll make it!" and "We'll be warm and dry soon!"

Finally she shouted back at him, "Shut-up and hurry!" So he did.

By the time they reached the clearing where the house was, the brutal wind had moved on and the sleet was just drizzle. Meyo stopped halfway across the clearing and breathed-out, "Oh no." Kelsey stepped sideways to see past her. One of the big pine trees, probably older and more brittle than the ones around it, had come down. So much for the wisdom of building in among the trees for shelter. The tree hadn't fallen straight onto the house, but one or two of its big branches had gashed along one of the side walls, tearing it open.

Kelsey had to untie Meyo's snowshoe bindings, because her fingers were too numb and shaking. He was soaked through and shivery, too, but he hadn't started out already half-frozen with sinkhole slush. He hadn't known that Indian lips could turn blue the same as white ones.

Inside, the gash along the side wall looked even worse than it had from outside. Some places were wide open from the roof peak to the ground, where the branches of the falling tree had torn away the poles holding the birchbark down. Everything was covered with sleet that was either soaking in or starting to freeze. Kelsey said to Meyo, "You find something warm and dry to wrap around you instead of those wet clothes. I'll get a fire going." She didn't argue or tell him that he should get into something dry too, before starting a fire. Which meant she was in even worse shape than he'd thought.

The live coals and ashes that should've been in the fire circle were just wet, dead, crumbly stones and cold mud. Kelsey scraped them aside to get a little patch of bare earth that was only moist, not wet, then reached for the birch bark rogan of crumbled punkwood and dried moss that they used for tinder. Inside was just a soggy mass. So he reached instead for the pile of twigs that should've been the second stage after the tinder caught. They were wet, too, but maybe if he broke them into tiny pieces so their dry insides were open, and made a little pile of them...

He did that, then sprinkled on a bit of gunpowder from his powder flask and struck a spark with his flint and steel. The gunpowder flared up, then flared out. The twig bits just sat there. Kelsey tried again. Same thing.

Meyo had found a merely-damp blanket to wrap around herself, instead of her sleet-soaked deerskin dress, and was hunkered on the other side of the fire circle. Her teeth were chattering and her big, dark eyes had an unhealthy sheen to them. Kelsey searched around frantically with his eyes and his mind, trying to think of something he could use to get a fire going. He was surrounded by birch bark, but it was all soaked through and iced over. Then he thought of something that would definitely be dry and would catch fire easily.

Kelsey rummaged in his pile of gear and came out with the waterproof oilskin packet wrapped around his journal — the journal that would show the Governor at York Factory how far he'd travelled and what a good job he'd made of the expedition he'd been sent on. He hadn't written in it since getting back to Deering's Point, since there wouldn't be any more journeying to record until the spring, so there were a few blank pages at the back. Kelsey tore them out and tore them into strips, threaded the bits of paper in among the bits of twigs, then tried the gunpowder and spark again. The paper caught and so did the twigs. He put a couple of larger twigs on top, but the ice water sizzling out of them started to drown the little flames coming up from the twig bits. Kelsey looked at Meyo shivering on the other side of the fire circle, then started to rip out pages he'd written on and feed them in. Pretty soon he had enough twigs and branch ends going to put on a full sized stick of firewood. The moisture sizzling out of it threatened to dampen the rest out, but the flames from the journal's pasteboard covers took care of that.

When the fire was well enough established to be left alone for a moment, Kelsey did what Meyo'd done: found a semi-dry blanket to replace his wet clothes. He and she sat side-by-side feeding the fire, each cocooned in their separate blanket. Once the fire was burning well, Meyo rearranged the blankets to make one double layer shawled across both their backs so their naked fronts were open to the heat.

Meyo eventually stopped shivering and Kelsey noticed her head angling around and up and down, looking at the shattered wall in front of them and the whole one behind and above them. She said, "I guess we don't have a wigwam anymore, but we sure do have one damn big lean-to." Kelsey laughed and kissed her lovely, flat-slanted cheek.

Actually they did have a wigwam again in a few days. They pirated enough birch bark and poles from the outer layer of the unbroken part of the torn wall to fill in the gaps. It meant that that section of the wall wasn't as well insulated now, but now the weather wasn't going to be as cold.

Spring came, bringing grey dots of pussy willow catkins along the creek and riverbanks, a silvery haze when the sunlight caught them right. In the Indian language they were "puppy willows," which made perfect sense to Kelsey once he realized that the only cat in the Indians' world was the uncuddly lynx. Spring also brought canoes full of Indians gathering to make the journey to the whiteskins' trading fort on the salt water. Soon Deering's Point—The Going-North Place—was covered with wigwams. Clawface showed up, as he'd said he would, and seemed to take it as a given that Kelsey would be going with him and the fleet of canoes to York Factory. Kelsey wasn't so sure.

On the surface, it seemed like the obvious and logical thing to do: go back and get the supplies and trade goods he would need for another year in the Indian lands, and then start west again with the canoe fleet heading for their homes. After all, the Governor had said at the start, "This expedition would be a year at least, perhaps two." But Kelsey would be appearing at York Factory without having met the Assinae Poets—the fabled, fierce and fur-rich tribe farther inland than the Naywatamee Poets—and without having made a peace so the inland natives could travel safely to the bay. The Indians he'd be bringing to York Factory would be just the same ones who went there every year.

He wouldn't even be bringing a written record of where he'd travelled last year—the journal that was so important to the Governor he didn't care Kelsey had no mapmaking skills. All in all, the Governor might well decide there was no point in sending him out for another year of failure, and "failure" was exactly the word that would be written beside The Company's record of Henry Kelsey. On the other hand, one more year and he could come back to York Factory with all the accomplishments that would put him high on The Company's list of bright young men. But to do that, he needed more supplies...

So what Kelsey decided to do was make a list of the things he would need, send the list with Clawface to York Factory and have Clawface and his men bring the things back to him. There were two problems with that plan. The first was that the Governor might find it strange that Kelsey was at the place the canoe fleet had started out from but hadn't come with them. The answer to that problem was that the Governor wouldn't know where Kelsey was, and Clawface could just tell the Governor he and Kelsey had arranged to meet somewhere inland—which wasn't exactly a lie. For all the Governor knew, Kelsey might've spent last winter much farther inland, maybe even with the Assinae Poets.

The other problem was that Kelsey had no paper to write a list on. He got Meyo to show him how to cut a long sheet of thin birch bark. Actually, she did it while he watched and lent a clumsy hand. It turned out, though, that pencils didn't work very well on birch bark. But one thing about cooking over wood fires, there was plenty of charcoal lying around.

It took Kelsey a while to make the list, balancing how much of what he would like to take west against how much could actually be carried in three or four canoes. When he checked the list over one last time, he remembered the time he'd been frantically reloading his rifle as the second grizzly bear charged up the hill, and the time he'd cocked his rifle in Meyo's family's camp and been wondering what he was going to do if he fired off his one shot and still had a bunch of angry relatives to deal with. And there'd been a number of other times in the past year when the Little Giant would've been very little indeed after firing off his one giant shot. He added to the list: *a brace of pistols*.

Not all of the Indians gathered at Deering's Point went off with the fleet. Most of the women and children and a few men stayed behind. Kelsey spent a lot of time smoking tobacco and drinking Indian tea with the men, learning what they knew of the Assinae Poets, although they pronounced it more like *Assiniboines*. When Meyo told him it meant "The People Who Cook With Stones," Kelsey said, "But...everybody cooks with stones, everybody without iron pots. *Your* people cook with stones." She just shrugged.

Kelsey began to get the idea that Meyo's people, and the people of old Seven Stars, *were* the Naywatamee Poets the Governor had spoken of. They didn't call themselves that, but then why would they call themselves anything except "us?" He decided he'd guessed right that "Naywatamee" had something to do with *nayok*: "the edge" or "the border." After all, Seven Stars and his people lived along the eastern edge of the grasslands, and Meyo's people on the western border of the woodlands. They were close together in language—kind of a blend. Out there on the buffalo plains, beyond the edges where Seven Stars and his people roamed, were the real Assinae Poets, but none of the men at Deering's Point had ever been that far west, or if they had they didn't want to talk about it.

Kelsey noticed that Meyo seemed to smile and laugh more with a camp full of other people around her, and other women to go foraging in the woods with. And he noticed something else about her. Even with all those other people around, she no longer walked with her head slightly stooped so her hair would cover the right side of her face. That made him smile.

The fleet came back from York Factory laden with all the wonderful and useful things they'd traded their furs for, and with everything on Kelsey's list, including a new, blank-paged journal notebook. Clawface said that the Governor had been pleased with the furs Kelsey had got in trade last winter and sent to York Factory with the fleet. Kelsey had made sure to add a full inventory of them to his list, so Clawface couldn't "accidentally" mix a few of them in with his own.

When he had a moment to himself, Kelsey sat down cross-legged by the fire with his new notebook, bent it open to the first page and carefully pencilled:

A Journal of a voyage & Journey undertaken
by henry Kelsey through Gods assistance
to discover & bring to a Commerce the
Naywatame poets in Anno 1691

Kelsey's expedition set off west this time with four canoes instead of three. And this time Kelsey wasn't just travelling with hired strangers; in the same canoe as him was Meyokwaiwin. And this time Kelsey wasn't just going far-ther west than any white man had gone, but farther than any Indian of this tribe. He found it comforting that despite the famous stone faced Indian reputation, he could tell they were just as scared as he was.

VIII

MEYO KNELT BEHIND THE MID-THWART, bending and dipping in time with the other three paddlers in the canoe. Kelsey was in front of the mid-thwart, and although his paddle stroke still wasn't as natural as people who'd been doing it all their lives it was getting close. Clawface was in the stern, and one of the men who'd travelled with him last year was in the bow. Several children too small to paddle were dotted between them. This year Kelsey's not-war party was more like any natural band of summer roamers, with some of the paddlers' wives and children coming along.

Meyo had been relieved and disappointed that the plan was to not travel as far by canoe this year. They were going to cache the canoes at a place where the river angled to the south and east, then head west on foot from there. That meant they wouldn't be following the river as far as where her family'd been camped last summer and might be again this summer.

Meyo wasn't sure how she'd feel when she some day met up with her family again, or how they'd feel. She missed them, but the last time she'd seen her father he'd been scheming to have Kelsey left alone on the prairie to wander lost and die. And the last time she'd seen her mother it had been a spitting face and grasping hands on the other side of the fishnet that had ended up helping to keep Meyo and Kelsey alive.

When the canoes were carried up from the river and covered with brush to *maybe* hide them from the eyes of other wanderers, the next problem was that the canoes had carried more things than the men and women who'd paddled them could carry on their backs. One of the things Kelsey's chief had sent him from the salt water was a big keg of gunpowder. Kelsey emptied half of it into deerskin bags, filled the space in the keg with knives and tobacco and other things—the iron things furled in a blanket so they wouldn't scrape together and spark—and they buried the keg beside a pink-streaked boulder. Now Meyo knew of two treasure caches, one in a tree and one in the ground,

As they set off on the path that would soon bring them to the western edge of the woodlands, Meyo found herself wondering about the good and bad sides of travelling by land or water. Two people in a canoe could bring a lot more things with them than two people walking, even if the walking ones had dogs to help them. But in a canoe you had to follow all the twists and windings of the river, which meant that in two days you might cover less distance than you could in one day walking in a straight line. But you couldn't walk a straight line in the woods anyway, there were always swamps and cliffs and thickets to swerve around. On the prairie you could walk in one direction from sunrise till sunset and find nothing in your way except maybe a ravine with a stream you could wade across easily. It seemed that the two different ways of travelling balanced out and were perfectly fitting for the two different kinds of country. Meyo'd noticed lately that almost everything that passed across her mind or her eyes seemed perfectly fitting and right in its own way. She had a feeling that that had more to do with something that was happening inside her than the things outside her. But she wasn't sure yet.

The cool, damp, musky smells of moss and pine gave way to sun-cured grass and sage. On the third day after leaving the river they made camp early so the men could spread out and hunt some food; the last of the smoked fish had been eaten that morning. The hunters came back with nothing but two grouse and one squirrel, which wasn't much for almost three tens of mouths, even if some of them were small. Meyo and some of the other girls and women had found a little pond nearby and dug some cattail roots, but that didn't make for more than a nibble all around. It was too early in the year for the small-headed sunflowers with the big orange roots. Maybe there were other plants on the prairie all around them that were good to eat, but Meyo and the other people of the woods didn't know them.

The next day they came across a campsite of the people of the plains, or the remains of one. The grass in the circles where the tents had been was still flattened down and brown, so the people hadn't been gone all that long. One of Clawface's men said he could follow the bruised-grass trail left by the dragging ends of the pack dogs' poles. So Kelsey went with that man and another and a boy, to catch up with the people who'd been camped there and bring back food. As the four of them set off, Meyo was pleased to see that Kelsey immediately fell into the same gait as the other three, that loose-legged wolf lope that ate up distance without eating up your lungs and muscles. Maybe he'd learned it from that Indian boy on his journey north along the shore of the salt water two years ago, that Kelsey'd told Meyo of in some of the long winter nights in the birch bark house on Deering's Point. Or maybe it just came natural to him.

After another hungry day, one of the men who'd gone with Kelsey came back with no food. He said he and Misstopashish had indeed caught up with the people from the camp, but those people turned out to be down to eating half-ripe berries and boiled bark. Their new camp, though, was close to a swampy lake where they hoped to get some ducks and maybe even a moose. Instead of waiting for maybe, this man had wanted to come back and try to hunt something for the ones who'd stayed behind, so they wouldn't starve to death before Kelsey could bring back food. Kelsey had given him some gunpowder and told him to get some shot from Meyo.

Meyo knew the man was telling the truth because he said Misstopashish had told him she would give him a "hap-duzz" lead balls, which was as close as he could come to Kelsey's "half-dozen." Over the winter she'd picked up many bits and pieces of Kelsey's language while he'd been getting better at hers. It was frustrating, though, with all its silly rules. In her language, the order of words was no big problem: "Up go that hill I'll there," was the same as "I'll go up that hill there."

The man who'd come back and asked Meyo for musket-balls signified something else to her, something about her that had changed, or the way other people saw her. Now, it seemed to be an understood thing that she was the keeper of Misstopashish's belongings when he wasn't there. What belonged to him belonged to her.

Neither she nor anyone else starved to death before Kelsey sent back the other man and the boy, with a quarter of a moose and a memory map of how to get to the camp where Kelsey had stayed. When they got there, Meyo picked out Kelsey's pale eyes flicking along the line of carriers, looking for her. When he saw her, his eyes stopped flicking but he just nodded and stayed standing where he was. She nodded back. They were both alive and in the same place and that was that.

They hadn't been at that camp long before five men from another tribe came in off the prairie. They came in from the west with the blazing sun behind them, so when first seen they were just dark, shimmering shadows that it hurt your eyes to look at for long, which didn't seem to Meyo like a good sign. But it turned out they were just messengers from old Seven Stars, who'd heard that Misstopashish had come back as he'd promised, and wanted him to meet him at a place called Waskashreeseebee. Or so they said.

The name of the place, Waskashreeseebee, made Meyo nervous, because she didn't know what it meant. *Waska* was the "around" part of a lot of words: *waskahikun*, "the house that is around you," or *waskakapowewuk*, "they stand around." But the rest of the name was in a language she didn't know, maybe the language of the far west Assiniboines, who were said to be harsher than the harsh plains they lived on. It might be that this message wasn't from Seven Stars at all, just bait to lure travellers loaded down with treasure into an ambush.

When she murmured her worry to Kelsey that night he didn't say she was just being a silly girl, but neither did he say they wouldn't go to Waskashreeseebee. He said, "Well, we have a dozen men with guns, some of us with more than one gun. I don't think there's any band of thieves around here as would care to take us on. As long as we keep our eyes open."

As long as she and Kelsey were murmuring in the night anyway, there was something else Meyo wanted to tell him, something that was maybe making her more worried and protective than she would normally be. But she wasn't sure yet.

Waskashreeseebee turned out to be a wooded ravine around a swelling in a little river—not the same ravine Seven

Stars said he'd be camped in again this summer. But Seven Stars was there, and seemed very happy to see Misstopashish. Naturally there was a feast, with Kelsey at the head of the circle and Meyo sitting beside him among the men in case he had trouble understanding what was said or making himself understood.

It didn't take Meyo long to figure out why Seven Stars indeed was truly very happy to see Misstopashish. Word would've spread very quickly that there were men from the woodlands with guns roaming onto the grasslands this summer. Last fall these same woodland men with guns, or ones like them, had raided a campful of Seven Stars's friends and relatives, and killed all those who couldn't run away. But as long as Kelsey was there, carrying his chief's commands to make a peace so that the people of the plains could bring their furs to the salt water, the men who'd got their guns from Kelsey or his chiefs wouldn't be using those guns on Seven Stars and his people.

After the feasting and drumming and singing, there was a lot of talking and passing the pipe back and forth, as Seven Stars and Clawface made speeches about the possibility of the buffalo people travelling safely through the woods people's territory to the whiteskins' trading place. Meyo didn't feel particularly useful, since Kelsey seemed to be having no particular trouble with her language or the slight differences in the way Seven Stars spoke it. A couple of times she wanted to say something to Kelsey in his own language, about a few things Clawface was exaggerating, but she didn't know how much English Clawface understood.

A strange sensation caught Meyo by surprise, a movement deep inside her belly that had nothing to do with all the buffalo meat she'd eaten. It wasn't much of a movement, something like the flutter of a sleepy moth cupped in your hands. But it was definitely there. She got up and moved away from the circle. A strange confusion of feelings had taken hold of her, happiness mixed with fear and several other things. She wandered through the camp, hoping no one would talk to her until the confusion passed, or at least settled down a little. She was glad that night had fallen, since as long as she stayed back from the campfires no one would notice her wiping her face or see the glint of tears.

There was enough room in the tipis of Seven Stars's camp for all the travellers to be parcelled out among them. But since it was a clear night, most had decided to sleep out under the stars. Meyo unrolled her and Kelsey's bed nearby one of the smudge fires built to keep the mosquitoes away, then walked around the camp some more, thinking of what to say and when and where to say it.

There was a full moon, so even when Meyo got out beyond the edge of the camp and the light of the campfires she could still see quite clearly, at least where the shadows of the trees weren't too thick. There was a place by the stream bank where a shelf of rock had kept trees from growing, so there were hardly any shadows at all. Meyo sat down on one of the mossy boulders for a moment, looked around and decided this would be as good a place as any. Then she went back and sat on the bed beside the smudge fire and waited.

She didn't have to wait for long. Feast-stuffed stomachs made for sleepy heads. Soon the men started getting up and drifting away from the council fire. Not that they were all talked out; they would start again tomorrow. A flicker of fire-light on sunflower coloured hair showed Meyo where Kelsey was ambling around wondering where she and his bed were. She stood up and called out, "Kelsey," not too loudly.

As he came up to her he said, "Are you all right? You left so sudden."

She half-whispered, "I have something to tell you," and angled her head toward the edge of the camp. Kelsey looked around, pale eyes suddenly wary, then bent down and picked up his two one-hand guns—no weapons around the council fire—and shoved them in his belt. But he left his rifle where it lay.

Once they got out past the last tipis, Kelsey said, "What is it?"

"Not yet. Just a little farther." When they got to the place she'd decided on, she sat down on the flat-topped mossy rock she'd tried out just a while ago. Kelsey stood looking around uncertainly, as though maybe there was something he was supposed to see. Meyo gave her hand a little downward wave, to say he might want to be sitting down for this. He found a handy rock a little ways in front of her and sat waiting, looking at her with his head cocked sideways and his thin forehead wrinkled. Kelsey's light bones and bright colouring had always reminded her a bit of a bird, and now more than ever.

Meyo had thought of a hundred different ways to say what she had to say, when and if the time came. Now that the time had come, she just said, "I'm pregnant."

Meyo had also thought of a hundred ways Kelsey might react, from jumping up happily to soft-voiced surprise. The one thing she'd never imagined was that his face would go stony and his eyes turn into glass beads staring past her. The cold, blue moonlight made his pointy features and pale eyes into something carved from milky ice. Eventually he said, "But...the child won't be able to have a name."

She blinked at him so hard her eyelids hurt. When she could find her tongue again she said, "Of course it will! A baby name at first, and then a child name."

"No..." He shook his head and seemed to be trying very hard to explain something, maybe to himself. "I mean a last name. An English child has no last name unless the parents have been married, in a *church*." He'd had to use the English word "church," since there was no word for anything like it in her language. Church was one of the English words she'd learned from him over the winter, though she hadn't been able to picture exactly what it meant. The best she could guess was that it was a sacred place, sort of like a sweat lodge but very different. "My last name—Kelsey—was my father's last name, or so I'm told."

"But no one here needs a last name. One name's enough, until it changes."

"But..." He was struggling, and she was getting the feeling he was trying to say what he meant without saying it. She wasn't sure whether the feeling was sad or mad, but it wasn't good. "But what if something happens to me? You'd be alone with a child to take care of."

"Nothing's going to happen to you."

He just shrugged at her with his shoulders, hands and scanty eyebrows. The shrug told her plainly that they both knew anything could happen to anybody at any time.

Meyo said, "I wouldn't be alone. I would go back with my family," they would have her back if she came crawling, "or join up with another family of my people." She didn't say she would likely become the third or fourth wife of some hunter who would put up with her flat-sided face for the sake of the work she could do, and for her knowing more about the white-faced traders and their language than anyone else around.

"But..."

Meyo thought that if Kelsey said "but" one more time she was going to hit him with a stick, or more likely a rock since there were more of them close at hand.

"But your child, our child—what would be just *your* child if something happened to me—you would have to look after it all by yourself, raise it and feed it and all."

That was confusing to Meyo. She said, "A child is everybody's child. If a child from someone else's wigwam wanders into mine when I'm cooking fish, I give it some fish. If my child curls up and falls asleep in someone else's wigwam, so what?"

"Huh." At least he hadn't said "but" this time. He was shaking his head slowly, with his lips pursed together, but not in a "no" kind of way. As Meyo waited to hear what "huh" meant, the peep and thrum of a nighthawk coasted over the burbling and rustling of the stream and trees. At last Kelsey said, "In my country, a woman as has a baby without being married is ruined. There ain't many ways open to her to feed herself and her child, and no matter what she does she's seen as a bad woman."

"That's crazy."

"Maybe it is, but that's the way it is. And sometimes the woman don't got any choice but to give up her child, put it in a place where a lot of the same kind of children grow up behind walls and trained to be...well, to be slaves."

"That's..." Meyo couldn't think of any other word for it but, "evil."

Kelsey just shrugged.

Meyo leaned forward to put her hand on his knee and said, "We're not in your country."

Kelsey said, "Huh," again, then nodded and smiled like the load that had settled onto his back had been lifted off. But not entirely. "But...my plan, *our* plan for this year was to maybe take up Seven Stars's invitation to go west with him and winter with the Assinae Poets. That's a lot of hard travelling and uncertainty. You'll be carrying a child."

"So?"

"Well, in my country, a woman carrying a child wouldn't go carrying a heavy packbasket all day long across the prairie. And when it got close to her time, she wouldn't go anywhere at all that wasn't close to her bed, and within calling distance of the medicine women that'll help her through the torture."

"The women of your country must be very weak indeed."

Kelsey laughed. Then he moved off his rock to crouch beside her and put his head in her lap, with one ear against her belly. She said, "I don't think there's anything to hear yet, except maybe my stomach growling at the buffalo it's caught," and twined her fingers in his hair, finer and silkier hair than she'd ever felt except a baby's.

They stayed in the ravine with Seven Stars and his band for some days, with the men spending much of those days talking around the council fire. Kelsey seemed pleased with the way the peace talk was going. Meyo wasn't so sure. She'd seen men make flowery promises to each other before, and flowers didn't last forever. It wasn't just a question of whether the buffalo people would be allowed to go in peace through the woodlands, carrying their furs to the whiteskins. Meyo knew there was another, unspoken question in the minds of Clawface and his men, because it was in her mind, too. It was one thing for the people of the plains to trust the woodland people to let them pass safely, but another thing for Meyo's people to trust that the buffalo people's war parties wouldn't use what their trading parties learned of the pathways and rivers all the way from the west edge of the woodlands to the shore of the salt water.

Seven Stars decided that this ravine and the prairie around it were getting fished out and hunted out for now, so it was time to move camp a bit farther west. Kelsey decided that since that was the direction he and his party were heading anyway, they might as well all travel together. After a few days of travelling—pretty slow travelling, what with dogs dragging tent poles and women carrying worn-out children—a scout came back and said there was a camp up ahead, a camp of what Kelsey called "Assinae Poets," but so far up ahead it would probably take another day for this plodding band to get there.

Meyo thought Kelsey might want to hurry on ahead. But instead he asked Seven Stars who his fastest runner was, then sat down and cut some tobacco. He gave the cut tobacco to the long-legged young man and told him one handful was his payment and the other handful was for the spokesman of the *Assinae Poets*. The tobacco gift was to ask them to keep camped where they were and wait.

At nightfall the runner came back. He said that as soon as he'd delivered the message the Assiniboines started to break camp and move on quickly. It seemed that in the spring they'd killed two woodlands women and were afraid that the woodlands men with guns were coming to get revenge.

That night, Meyo was jerked awake by Kelsey's sputtering and cursing and flailing. It took her eyes a moment to clear enough to see what was going on. Kelsey was up on his knees batting a moccasin at the smudge fire. But no, it wasn't the smouldering smoky smudge fire, it was clear flame. The wooden stock of his rifle was on fire.

Once the fire was put out—thanks to a birch bark water bottle Meyo hoped they'd get a chance to refill soon—Kelsey said, "My own damn fault. Look, there was this patch of moss beside the smudge fire, and I went and laid my gunstock down right on top of it—sooner or later the moss was bound to get dried out enough to pass the fire along. Oh well, soon as we get to a place with decent trees I'll just carve me another piece of gunstock and patch it together. No real harm done, just a stupid accident."

Meyo wasn't so sure, but didn't say so. She couldn't remember whether that *was* exactly where Kelsey had laid down his rifle. And she had a notion that if the wooden gunstock had burned all the way up to the metal part of the rifle, the gunpowder inside it would've exploded, right beside Misstopashish. After Kelsey'd gone back to sleep, she sat up thinking. She wasn't thinking just for herself anymore, or even just for her and Kelsey.

In the morning, when the camp was awake but not yet on the move again, she murmured to Kelsey, "Don't you think Clawface and the others will want to get back to their families before winter sets in? They got a long ways to go. There's enough other people here to carry all your trade things, and there'll be less to carry once you've paid out some of your things to Clawface and them for coming this far."

Kelsey's eyes went sideways toward where Clawface and his people were rolling up their beds and getting ready for the day. It seemed to Meyo that Clawface was already glancing sideways at Kelsey and her, as if he knew something was in the wind.

Meyo added in an even lower murmur, "Clawface and them can't be much help to us from here on anyway. None of them can talk the Assiniboine language any better than we can. Seven Stars can."

Kelsey's eyes went narrower and he chewed on his lower lip, something he tended to do when he was thinking on something. Then he headed over toward Clawface. Meyo busied herself with her packbasket, keeping half an eye on

Kelsey and Clawface. After some while Kelsey came back and told her that Clawface had decided to go no farther west; he would meet Misstopashish again at Deering's Point next spring when the rivers were clear of the ice that would start setting in soon.

Something occurred to Meyo only after the people who'd camped together last night set off in two separate directions, some to the east and most to the west. It was something she hadn't thought of when she'd been thinking of how to get Clawface and his friends travelling in a different direction from her and Kelsey. The thing Kelsey had said to make her feel safer—back when she was worried that the message claimed to be from Seven Stars might be a trap—was no longer true. They were no longer travelling with a dozen men with guns, just Kelsey, and his rifle had a burned-off stock that wouldn't fit to his shoulder.

IX

KELSEY WAS WALKING IN THE FRONT ROW of the fanned-out travelling line—loosely four or five abreast, including dogs dragging pack poles—between Meyo and Seven Stars, when Meyo did a little crossover step to get around behind him and over to his other side. She murmured to Seven Stars, not loud enough for the rest of the band to overhear but Kelsey did, "We're not alone."

Seven Stars murmured back, "Haven't been for some while now."

She hissed, "I thought they were your friends?"

"Haven't killed us, have they? Yet."

Kelsey glanced around uncomfortably. All he could see was tall grass in all directions, gone a less succulent green in the dusty autumn winds, but apparently there was someone out there—several someones. He had his loaded rifle slung over his shoulder but it was virtually useless, still with its stock burned down to a charred nub. Since the campfire accident they'd sometimes camped in islands of poplar trees with trunks wide enough to make a new stock, and plenty of deadfalls, but green wood was liable to warp and deadwood liable to have veins of rot. And then there'd been a week when they saw no trees at all, just short dry grass and spiky brush. When he'd added up those days in his journal, the barren ground had lasted forty-six miles. More or less. The miles had begun to run together and Kelsey was beginning to wonder if his best guesses were maybe not so good. Seven Stars assured him they were heading for the wintering rendezvous with the Assiniboines, but some days it seemed like headless wandering.

Kelsey's near-useless rifle, though, didn't leave him feeling unarmed and naked. He was carrying the short-barrelled musket that he'd usually kept loaded with birdshot but lately with a musketball, and had a brace of pistols in his belt. He might as well be unarmed and naked, though, if arrows suddenly started darting from nowhere in the tall grass. He looked around for something else to think about.

There was something else, up ahead, smoke rising toward the few clouds in the sky. Very far up ahead, but a lot of it. Kelsey said to Seven Stars, "Prairie fire?" From what Kelsey'd heard, prairie fires were more fearsome than any human enemy.

Seven Stars said, "No, no—just the campfires of the wintering place in the Ochre River Valley."

So as they walked along, Kelsey peered ahead for the appearance of some hazy hills that would have a valley between them. Come sunset he still didn't see any hills although the smoke seemed to be getting a lot closer—grey plumes now black against the incandescent red of the western sky—but distances were hard to judge on the plains. Then a zigzag crack opened up in the Earth and grew wider and wider as he got closer till he was standing on the edge of it looking down. Seemed that valleys on the prairies weren't between hills, but gaps that rivers carved into the flat land on either side. Down below him were a hundred or so cone-shaped, painted buffalo hide tents on either side of a ribbon of river, sheltered from the wind that would scour across the open plains all winter long.

Seven Stars started down a narrow path snaking toward the camp. Kelsey followed him and Meyo, and the others fell in behind. A cloud of sound billowed up the valley wall: hundreds of day's-end human voices and almost as many dogs, the thunking of stone axes into firewood, and then the deep booming of a drum in a slow, steady rhythm. When Kelsey and Seven Stars reached the bottom of the path, a delegation was coming out to meet them—tattooed men with painted faces and feathered spears—and escorted them to the centre of the camp where several older men in feathered headdresses and horned buffalo crown hats were sitting on buffalo robes.

Seven Stars introduced Misstopashish with a long speech in the Assiniboine language, which seemed to be a different proposition entirely from the language he spoke with Meyo's people, then translated what they said in reply. During the speechifying, Kelsey watched to see which one of the older men the others looked to for cues, then murmured to Meyo, "The red coat..." She beckoned one of the other women forward, dug into that woman's packbasket and came out with the red wool, brass-buttoned presentation coat the Governor'd included in the spring supplies.

While Meyo was doing that, Kelsey got a chance to notice how she was presenting herself to the Assiniboines. At one of the afternoon rest stops she'd changed into the fancier of the two grown-woman dresses she'd made over the winter from deerskin and Kelsey's trade samples, the one with bright-beaded black velvet on the yoke front and back. It was lucky that Indian dress patterns—sleeves and yoke one piece; breast-high, shoulder-strapped skirt another—left room for expansion, because Meyo's breasts and belly were a good deal larger than even a month ago. She seemed totally oblivious that her face was shaped any different from other women's, so if it drew any stares it was just because it wasn't painted orange with ochre like many of the women around the council circle.

Seven Stars seemed a little miffed when Kelsey presented the coat, but Seven Stars had had plenty of other presents in the past and would get more in the future. Kelsey was more concerned with seeing whether he'd picked the right one among the five senior men on their buffalo robes, and it seemed he had. One thing Kelsey'd learned was that the chain of command in the Indian world was a lot more fluid than the white world, if the notion of command even existed at all.

Another thing he'd learned was that the name one tribe had for another wasn't necessarily the name they called themselves—you could end up calling people Thieving Snakes or Scalp-eaters. He couldn't see anything particularly insulting about Cook With Hot Stones, but insults were in the ear of the insulted. So one of the first things he picked out from the back and forth between Seven Stars and the Assiniboines was that they called themselves "Nakota."

With the preliminaries done with, Kelsey spread out a blanket for him and Seven Stars to sit on while proceeding with the getting-acquainted. Which of course included more presents. First was an iron pipe bowl with an ornamental hatchet head tailpiece. The Nakota presented Misstopashish with a pipe bowl in return. It was unlike any pipe Kelsey had seen before, made of milky-waved green marble and not carved into any ornamental shape and no need to—amazing enough that they'd managed to carve marble so thin with only stone tools. So thin that after sunset the Nakotas' marble and bluestone pipes glowed from inside when puffed.

There was a feast, of course, and when the feasting was done one of the Nakota chiefs started pointing at Kelsey's feet and saying something insistent. Seven Stars said, "They want us to take our moccasins off."

"Why?"

Seven Stars shrugged, so Kelsey just did as he was told. Two Nakota women came forward with scrolls of birch bark, unrolled the scrolls and drew charcoal outlines of their bare feet. Kelsey wanted to tell them Meyo already had moccasin patterns for him, but when in Rome...

Kelsey didn't have long to wait to find out why. Two days later, one of the Nakota chiefs came to the edge of camp where the people who'd come with Kelsey and Seven Stars had put up their tents—Seven Stars had said it wouldn't be the edge of camp long, as more wanderers came in off the plains to the wintering place. The grey-haired Assiniboine brought two pairs of moccasins unlike any Kelsey had seen before, standard toe piece and body of soft leather but with a second sole of thicker rawhide sewn onto the bottom. Kelsey could see the sense of them for walking the plains, where your feet didn't have to feel and adjust to hummocky ground and tree roots but where the flat ground was liable to be studded with sharp pebbles and burs.

The moccasins turned out to be just a side reason for the visit. The leather-faced Nakota explained himself slowly, periodically adding a gesture of the universal hand-sign language when it fit with one of his words. Kelsey appreciated that, since it gave him a chance to fit the Nakota word to a meaning and slot it away in his language bin. The gist was that tomorrow most of the men in the camp were leaving at dawn on a buffalo hunt, and they were welcome to come. Scouts had spotted a herd less than half a day from camp—Seven Stars translated, "Not a big herd, maybe four tens of tens"—if it didn't move on before tomorrow. The invitation seemed to have a bit of a dare in it.

After the visitor had gone, Seven Stars said to the pair of moccasins in his hand, "If I'd wanted to wear prairie moccasins I would've got one of my wives to make me some. My feet are too old and hard to fret about a few small stones."

Kesley said, "I'd feel better about going buffalo hunting if my rifle was workable."

"Oh, you won't need your long-shooting gun for this kind of hunting, your shorter gun will do just fine."

Meyo said, "What kind of hunting?"

"In close. Me, I'm too old for that kind of thing."

Meyo said, "What kind of thing?"

"A lot of running around, and maybe running away."

Meyo looked at Kelsey like this maybe wasn't such a smart idea. Smart or not, he had a feeling he'd better go along if he hoped to get the Assinae Poets to listen to what the Governor wanted him to say. Before dawn, a big drum started thumping a slow heartbeat from the centre of camp. Kelsey quickly got himself dressed, with his shot pouch and powder flask crisscrossed from his shoulders. Seven Stars had said he should maybe bring a blanket, so he'd rolled and tied one with a rawhide thong last night, ready to sling on his shoulder. He picked up his carbine musket and stooped halfway out of the tipi, then had a second thought and stooped back in, scooped up his pistols and shoved them in his belt.

A lot of men and older boys—Kelsey guessed at least a hundred—were gathering in the centre of the camp. Kelsey didn't have a translator and sign talk was only good for pretty basic things, but he figured whatever'd have to be communicated wouldn't have many nuances and anyway he should likely just do what everybody else was doing.

They set off at a loping jog in three long lines. Kelsey joined up the end of the line that seemed the shortest. The sun had climbed about four times its width when they halted—not exactly a half-day's journey, but then again he hadn't seen any buffalo yet. One line peeled off to the left, another to the right, Kelsey's line just fanned out on either side of its leader. Kelsey ended up at the right-hand end of the fanned-out line and looked to see how much distance the man on his left had put between himself and the man on *his* left: about a hundred long paces—well, long for Misstopashish, anyway. They all hunched down and started moving forward silently.

After long enough for Kelsey's knees and back to start complaining about walking at a half-crouch, the man on his left stood up and started yelling, waving a sheet of rawhide over his head. And now there was a man on Kelsey's right—he'd thought he was the right end of the line—doing the same. So that was why Seven Stars had said to bring a blanket. But all the men were still striding forward while they shouted and flapped; if he stopped to put down his musket and unwrap his blanket he'd leave a gap in the line. So he just waved his musket over his head and joined in the shouting. It didn't seem to matter what exactly got shouted, just as long as it was loud.

As they moved forward, the man on Kelsey's left and the one on his right started to get closer to him and he realised what was going on. He was part of a wide, wide circle of hunters surrounding the herd and now gradually working their way in, tightening the circle. But what the shouting and flapping was supposed to accomplish was another question. Maybe frighten them to death?

From somewhere up ahead came a drumming that grew louder than all the Indian drums Kelsey had ever heard, thumping all together. A wide plate of dust appeared, and under it a black-brown, bawling, roaring, churning mass pounding toward him. As it got closer he began to see black gleams of shiny horns and hooves and white-rimmed eyes, all charging straight at his side of the circle. His first inclination was to throw down his musket and run—run where?—but the men on either side of him just kept yelling and waving, so he did the same. Amazingly, the buffaloes in the front rank turned to their right and the rest followed, galloping around the inside rim of the circle. The man on Kelsey's right kept on flapping and shouting, but the one on his left—still shouting—threw down his rawhide flag and fitted an arrow to his bow, so Kelsey lowered his musket and levelled it to take aim.

Aim at what? They were moving so fast and so jumbled together, if he tried for a heart shot he might just hit a leg. He decided if he just held the barrel at a slight angle down from his shoulder and pulled the trigger when a horn passed his sights, the ball might hit just behind the shoulder. When he fired, he saw a buffalo fall sideways and then disappear as the others jumped over it or swerved around. By the time he'd reloaded, the herd had passed, but then came around again as they ran around the circle in a panic trying to find a way out. He fired again and thought he'd brought down another. But the third time around one of the leaders swerved and charged straight toward him.

The men on either side of Kelsey dropped their bows and ran to left and right as the rest of the herd followed the one trying to break out; Kelsey was stuck in the middle. The logical part of his brain detached itself to observe that it only made sense for the bowmen to run—although it might be easy to turn a herd by bringing down the leader, a buffalo coming straight at you gave you nothing to shoot at but its massive head, and although Indian bows could drive an arrow amazingly hard and fast, buffalo skulls were amazingly thick. While Kelsey's mind was making that observation, his hands were throwing down his musket, drawing both pistols out of his belt, cocking them with the sides of his hands, aiming straight ahead point blank and pulling both triggers.

The lead buffalo somersaulted forward. Kelsey skipped out of the way of the cartwheeling hooves as the rest of the herd decided this wasn't a safe way to go so swerved back to stampeding along the circle of hunters. But this time when the tail end of the herd passed, the head didn't come around again and the booming and bellowing faded away, so Kelsey guessed one of them must've finally broken out and the rest of the living ones had followed, leaving their dead behind.

Now that it was over, Kelsey slumped to the ground, ears filled with the silence of the prairie winds. It occurred to him that the Governor would consider he'd done a good day's work, since the Indians had just been given a pretty good demonstration of why guns were handy things to have: worth trading a lot of furs for.

Another procession arrived from the camp in the valley, this time mostly women—including Meyo, who seemed bound and determined to prove that being pregnant didn't mean being incapacitated. The women went to work skinning buffalo and cutting meat into strips to hang on smoke-curing, sun-drying racks, while the men gorged on buffalo liver and kept away the camp dogs and the wolves that always lurked around the edges of buffalo herds. It seemed the plan was to camp at the killing grounds till all the butchering and meat-curing was done, which Kelsey figured was another reason Seven Stars had advised him to bring a blanket along. He was glad to see Meyo'd brought one too, so they had one for under and one for over.

By the time winter came, the tipi village in the valley had grown to a good-sized town. Misstopashish spent many days in many different tents giving presents and telling the buffalo people that the Governor wouldn't trade with them unless they stopped killing his friends the canoe people. Which always led around to the question and answer that, yes, once the Nakota were the Governor's friends he wouldn't keep on trading with the woodland people if they kept killing his friends the prairie people.

One midwinter evening in the big tipi Kelsey and Meyo shared with Seven Stars and some of his wives and children and grandchildren—others were in the tents on either side—Meyo stood up carefully and said, "I think it's time."

Seven Stars's youngest wife jumped up to help Meyo stoop out the doorway; his oldest wife picked up a large shoulder pouch and stood to follow them. Dim-struck Kelsey realised they were going out into the wind and snow and moved to stop them, saying, "No, you can't—" but then something hard whacked against the side of his stomach and stayed there. He looked down. It was the end of Seven Stars's walking staff, stretched out and angled to stop him.

Seven Stars said, "They are just going to another tent. It's been arranged."

"But—"

"It's woman's business now. You did the man's part, such as it is."

Kelsey looked around and couldn't think of anything else to do but sit back down. Seven Stars took out his long

Alfred Silver

stemmed pipe and methodically packed it and lit it to pass
back and forth. His oldest unmarried daughter sprinkled
some rosehips and herbs onto a small pot of water and set it
on the fire for tea.

Kelsey's fingers kept twisting together and picking at
his lower lip or rubbing his forehead. He was a child again,
on the backstreets of London, put out of the house and told
he'd be told when he could come back in. Even with all the
street noise of people and horses and carts, he could hear
his mother screaming. He'd walk what seemed like miles
through twisty alleys and open markets, but when he came
back she was still screaming. Meyo could say all she wanted
about it being different for Indian women, it wasn't always.
Over the autumn and winter, with so many people camped in
one place for so long, there'd naturally been more than a few
childbirths in the neighbourhood. And, yes, more often than
not the woman just went away from where the men were for
an hour or so and came back with a baby in her arms. But
two or three times in the winter he'd heard of complications
that'd drawn things out, and one time both the woman and
baby died and the whole camp mourned.

Sitting trying not to think beyond the tent walls, Kelsey
found himself wishing that the Indians had included alcohol
among all the wonderful things they'd learned to make from
the plants around them. A big mug of ale right now, or a
tumbler of brandy, would've helped the helpless time pass. As
it was, he figured he'd better find something to do with his
hands before he picked his face to pieces.

Among the paraphernalia stacked by his and Meyo's
rolled up bed was the embryonic beginnings of a new shoulder stock for his rifle. When winter had sucked all the sap out
of the trees, he'd found a scrub oak with a bend in the trunk

sort of vaguely like a rifle stock. He'd sectioned it out with axe and saw and now, after weeks of evening carving by the tipi firepit, it'd been whittled down to a slab of oak instead of a piece of tree. He rummaged it out and drew his belt knife and went slowly to work, being careful with shaky fingers.

Even with taking his turn at puffing the pipe, and sipping soothing tea, and concentrating on taking shavings off the wood and not his fingers, the time squeezed slowly by. Then Kelsey heard a strange sound, a high-pitched squalling approaching the tent. Meyo stooped inside looking a bit tired and sweaty but glossy-eyed, holding a washed and wrinkled new-minted human being wrapped in a rabbit blanket and looking like a skinned rabbit. Kelsey jumped up but then just stood there, overcome with awe. Meyo said, "Her father must carry her outside, not for long, just long enough to… First thing your eyes light on will be her name, till she gets old enough to earn another."

Kelsey did what he was told, holding the swaddled baby like a basket of eggs with no straw. As he stood up in the cold outside the tipi, his eyes were drawn upward. The Aurora Borealis, the Spirit Dance, was shimmering and shifting sheafs of blue and green above the valley. When he stepped back inside the tent, Meyo was looking a question at him. He said, "Wawatawin," her language for the Northern Lights. Well, Wawa was close to Aurora, which was the name he held in his mind.

Meyo nodded and said, "Now we are a family, Misstopashish." An ominous boulder of responsibility settled between Kelsey's shoulder blades, but the next instant Meyo was saying with delight, "Look at her face!"

Kelsey looked down at the white fur-wreathed head in the crook of his arm. Not much face to see: tiny nub of a nose, closed eyes, rosebud mouth... Meyo delicately drew one fingertip down the round, right contour of Aurora's face, then did the same on the left side and whispered, "See? The same."

"Ah," Kelsey whispered back. "Yeah, too bad she'll never be as lovely as her mother, but..." Meyo pinched the end of his nose between two knuckles and gave it a twist.

Springtime came to the prairies in a different way than Kelsey had ever seen before, or smelled. Different from York Factory or Deering's Point or back in England. Furry little purply blue and yellow flowers were pushing their heads up through the snow, and the air was tasty with the balsamy spicy smell of the trees coming back to life. He was sitting wrapped in his buffalo robe with his back against a twisted tree on the rim of the valley where he'd spent the winter.

He had his rifle propped across his knees, with its unartistic but serviceable new gunstock he'd spliced onto the unburnt part with many rounds of wet rawhide that shrunk tight when it dried. But he wasn't planning to shoot anything. He was supposedly gone hunting, but he didn't really expect to spot any game so close to the sounds and smoke of such a big camp whose hunters had been working the surrounding area all winter long. The signs of spring had told him it was time to get away from the bustle of the camp for a while, to sit down and get his bearings, get a handle on where he'd been and where he was going next and how to get there.

Oddly though, the longer he sat there the less he thought about Henry Kelsey, and more about bigger things. Sitting on the rim of the world with the sun on his face and no sound but the early spring breezes, he had a moment to consider the blasphemous notion that had seeped into him over the last two winters and the summers in between. Literally blasphemous—back in civilization, people had been burned at the stake for less. The notion was that maybe human beings weren't above and beyond, weren't wholly different from all the other living things on the planet. Maybe the differences were just in details and ways of living. The tree he had his back against couldn't get up and move away like he could, but he couldn't draw his food out of the earth and the sun. A wolf couldn't fire his rifle, but he couldn't smell a caribou half a mile away.

Another thing he couldn't do, he realized, was stay sitting where he was much longer without starting to shiver. The sun might be warmer than it had been a month ago, but it still wasn't warm enough to melt the snow all around him. The buffalo robe wasn't quite wide enough to fully overlap in front of him, and the long buckskin hunting shirt Meyo had made for him didn't insulate like wool—although it was a lot stronger, and soft as velvet. When he'd told her not to fuss too much with decoration, she'd patiently explained to him that the line of rawhide fringes across the chest and back, and the clumps at the shoulders, weren't just decoration. Rainwater would drip down the fringes and fall off, instead of soaking into the shirt. And if he suddenly had a need for a bit of rawhide thong to tie or bind something when he was out hunting, he could just yank off one of the fringes, or three or four and knot them together. When a hunter'd had to do that enough times that his fringes grew sparse, his wife would cut and sew a new line on, same as when the soles of his moccasins wore out she would take them apart and sew the old, beaded or quillworked toe pieces onto new soles.

As Kelsey made his way back down to the big camp on the valley floor, he realized that he and Meyo couldn't stay sitting where they were much longer, either. The message he'd asked Clawface to spread around through the winter was that, come the Birds' Eggs Moon, Misstopashish would lead a fleet of canoes from Deering's Point to York Factory. Not that Kelsey felt competent to lead or guide any of the people of the country anywhere in their country. But those who'd been hesitant about going to the white man's fort might feel better if a white man was going with them. If he hoped to be at Deering's Point before the Indians started showing up he'd have to start soon.

He'd also have to hire carriers to get his things across the prairie to the woodlands, and one more carrier than he would've needed in the fall, since Meyo's back-basket would be replaced by Wawatawin/Aurora's cradleboard. Most of Kelsey's baggage now was furs: beaver, fox, sable and a few buffalo robes. Almost all of his trade goods had been traded off over the winter, except what he and Meyo needed for their own use and a few things he would use to pay the carriers. Seven Stars pointed out the best men and women for the job, but said he wouldn't be going with them. He would stay behind awhile to put together a trading party and would surely be at the Going North Place before it came time to start north.

The night before they were due to leave, as Meyo was settling Wawatawin into the moss-lined niche on Meyo's side of the bed, Kelsey murmured sleepily, "Maybe she'll sleep right through the night again."

Meyo said mock-bitchy, "As if it makes any difference to *you*," then turned to look directly at him and turned more serious. "If your daughter was in danger—maybe fell in the river, or grabbed by a wolf—and some man rescued her, just a stranger passing by, would you feel a debt of gratitude to that man?"

"Huh? Of course. Who wouldn't?"

"And if that man got into trouble some day, was in danger, would you help him, stand beside him?"

"I should hope so. If I could. Why, uh...?" he struggled to work his sleep-numb mouth. "Why d'ya ask?"

"Just asking. Just wondering." She shifted her eyes to the low, dancing flames in the firepit and didn't seem inclined to say any more. Kelsey shrugged to himself and rolled over. He'd learned that no matter how many miles they travelled together, he and Meyo were of a different race and species and some things just wouldn't translate—parts of the land of female would always be a dark continent to male explorers.

X

WHEN MEYO HEADED EAST from the wintering valley with her man and her child and a dozen hired carriers, they were walking on snowshoes and towing laden toboggans. Well, all except Wawatawin on Meyo's back—it'd be another year or so before she walked on any kind of shoes. By the time they reached the western border of the woodlands the snow was gone and the toboggans and snowshoes cached for the carriers to pick up on their way back west.

Meyo looked at the tangled forest wall in front of her, knowing that the kind of thing she was looking for would be either a ways to the north or the south, one way as good as another. She decided that south would be more likely to find the path she and Kelsey had travelled two years back, back to the place her family often camped in summer, so she turned north. After a ways they came to a place along the wall that looked no less overgrown than any other, except that down among the leafy shadows on the ground was a small, round stone on top of a flat stone. Meyo pushed some brush aside and there was the beginning of the path.

Kelsey said, "Funny thing, two years ago it still wouldn't've looked to me like a path, even after you'd opened it up. But

even a slim stretch of unthicketed ground isn't there by accident, is it?"

Meyo said in English words—some of the carriers had
at least a few words of her own language—"No need so loud
talk." Next thing you knew, he'd be blurting out some of the
tricks her people used to tell each other that the path which
seemed to end in the middle of nothing would start up again
just over that way. Kelsey blushed a bit pink but nodded that
he understood.

As they moved onto the path, Meyo noticed that the buffalo people carriers were changing. Their shoulders grew
hunched and their eyes flicked worriedly from side to side
in this closed-in world of shifting shadows and tangled trees.
Not far into the woods, Meyo called a halt in a little clearing—actually not much more than a slight swelling of the
path. She told Kelsey to pay off the carriers and have them
leave their burdens there.

Kelsey looked at her sideways, like how did she plan to
get those bales of furs and all to a place where they could load
them into a canoe, or how to get a canoe for that matter? She
looked back at him levelly and instead of arguing he just gave
his last few extra axe heads and knife blades to the carriers as
presents to send them on their way. The buffalo people didn't
seem at all reluctant to go back out into the sunlight and keep
on going.

After the carriers were gone, Meyo asked Kelsey to fire
his rifle into the air, and his pistols. She picked up the smooth
bore carbine he kept loaded with birdshot and did the same.
Then she lifted aside a deadfall branch that appeared to've
just landed by happenstance on one edge of the little clearing—except that the long, brown needles were pine and the
only evergreens nearby were short-needled spruces. Under

the pine branch fan was a circle of old ashes surrounded by a shallow depression in the ground. Meyo picked up a round stone that just happened to be lying nearby and set it into the hand's-width trench. Kelsey said, "Ah," and Meyo saw him seeing that there were other stones like it lying here and there among the spruce and poplar roots. So anyone who knew the signs of this place could build a safe campfire quickly, and anyone who didn't know wouldn't know anyone had ever camped here.

Kelsey started to help Meyo fetch stones and set them around the fire circle. Once she saw he'd caught on, she asked him to finish the circle and make a fire. Then she hung Wawatawin's cradleboard from a handy hook where a spruce branch had broken off, and she went off into the woods. When she came back, Kelsey'd managed to get a fire going and she had a pouch full of the new green shoots that were the best thing about this time of year in the woods. She put the cast iron skillet on the fire, layered in some smoked buffalo meat and waited till it was sizzling before adding in the green shoots.

Kelsey said, "Looks like a lot of food for just the two of us. I don't think Wawatawin's up for solid food yet."

"No, she isn't."

A voice came out of nowhere, "Wachiye." Kelsey jumped up and started to reach for his rifle, but Meyo shook her head so he pulled his hand back.

Meyo called back calmly, "Wachiye," so Kelsey did, too. A large man with a bear claw necklace and empty hands stepped out of the woods. Meyo had a feeling there were others watching from the woods, and their hands weren't empty. She said, "I am Meyokwaiwin, daughter of Morning Wolf. And he is Misstopashish."

The man tapped his chest and said, "*Nunimiskum*," which meant "He Goes Against The Wind."

"Food's ready."

Against The Wind waved one hand over his shoulder and three other men stepped out of the woods, unnocking their bowstrings and putting the arrows back in their quivers. The four hunters squatted around the fire circle and everyone took out their own short-handled, big-bowled spoons decorated with the owner's totem or a few small feathers. Meyo's and the others' spoons were made from carved and hollowed out tree burls, Kelsey's from a buffalo horn. In between the polite belches and comments to show the cook her food was appreciated, the men's conversation moved in the usual circles of how hard or not-so-hard the last winter had been, whether the coming summer looked to be a good one and what kinds of funny accidents had happened to somebody's cousin lately. It was just talk that didn't mean much to anybody, and wasn't meant to, until one of the hunters mentioned he'd heard that Morning Wolf's first wife—Meyo's mother—had recently borne another daughter.

For no reason Meyo could call sensible, or no *one* particular reason, Meyo felt a choke in her throat and looked away from the others as though just concentrating on chewing a particularly tough chunk of buffalo.

Once the frying pan had been scraped clean, Meyo got hold of herself and got down to business. She took out the mid-sized cooking pot that had been with them since Deering's Point and said, "Misstopashish and me need to get all our furs and things carried to the little river on the other side of the black rock ridge. There, we will need a canoe big enough to carry all these things but small enough for two people to paddle. If someone could do that for us, we would gladly give that someone this iron cooking pot."

She noticed Kelsey looking boggle-eyed at her; that pot and the frying pan were the only two pieces of iron cookery they had left. She said to him in English, and flatly enough that the others wouldn't take a meaning from her tone, "I can water in pan boil as good like pot." After all, he could get plenty more, couldn't he?

The hunters murmured amongst each other, hands shielding their mouths. The look that Kelsey tossed at her this time had one pale, thin eyebrow raised. Just a quick glance, but she knew him well enough by now to read it as, "Okay, fine, but I don't get how they're gonna divide one pot between the four of them." She could explain it to him later, though she was surprised she'd have to. Maybe he'd spent too much time in the big camps of the buffalo people to understand that her people's small bands were like families, whose canoes and such belonged to all of them. Or maybe Kelsey did understand well enough to know that those "families" didn't always last forever, and then things like canoes and cooking pots got complicated. Well, if that happened someday with this band, that would be another day and far away. What mattered today was whether Against The Wind and his friends would take the trade.

Three mornings later Kelsey and Meyo set off in a laden canoe with Wawatawin's cradleboard nestled in among the rows of furs. Once they'd paddled far enough to get used to it again, Kelsey said over his shoulder, "Along the way we'll stop and dig up the cache we buried last summer...?"

It took Meyo a moment to remember what he was talking about: the barrel half-filled with gunpowder and half with blanket-wrapped trade goods. Only ten moons ago but that had been a different Meyokwaiwin, one who wasn't a mother. She said, "The river we landed the canoes from last summer nearby the pink rock where we buried the barrel, that river is a limb of this river—joins up a day or so from here. So to get to the barrel cache we'd have to sidetrack and then backtrack, and you did want to get to Deering's Point before everybody gives up waiting for you, didn't you?"

Kelsey said, "Hmm."

"Besides, where we gonna put a barrelful of things in a canoe that's already so heavy-loaded it can barely float?"

If Kelsey murmured anything in reply, she couldn't hear it over the murmur of the river. But his shoulders shrugged, and his head nodded, and he kept on paddling forward.

Meyo said, "The barrel cache'll stay safe a long time where it is, and I know how to find it again. Same goes for the canvas cache we nested in a pine tree two summers ago. Both will still be there when we pass this way again." There was that unsensible little choke in her throat again. She swallowed it and said, as much to herself and the river as to Kelsey, "When will that be?"

"Well...I can't say when, but seems logical-like to say it *will* be, in not all that long. Now as one of The Company's people has travelled far inland and come back safe—knocking wood..." He stopped paddling long enough to let go his right hand and rap its knuckles on the paddle, just one of those strange white man superstitions. "...seems only logical The Company'll send out another little expedition every year or two, to encourage more and more Indians to bring their furs to the bay. And it seems only logical Henry Kelsey'd be the lad to lead those expeditions. Maybe after we spend the winter at York Factory, you and me and Wawatawin'll be back in a canoe next summer heading west. Winter at York Factory... Huh."

"Huh what?"

"Huh? Oh, just... Funny thing, this river's gotten to be almost familiar to me, after three times up or down it in the last two years." It seemed to Meyo that wasn't exactly what he'd *Huh*ed about, but he went on, "Current seems faster and stronger'n I remember from before."

"It is, from all the melted snow."

"Oh, right, spring runoff—shoulda thoughta that. Well, lucky we're travelling downstream. Whup, watch out for them ripples up on the left, I think the high water's hiding something."

"I see no ripples."

"Oh, well, looked like it to me..."

The higher water also meant that some places they'd had to bypass overland before would now float the canoe, although Kelsey still didn't seem all that comfortable with shooting white water rapids. But most of the time the river was calm enough that Meyo could safely let her eyes drift to the shorelines passing by. Spring came more slowly to the shadowed woodlands than the plains; there were still bits of snow here and there, and the rabbit she caught in a snare by one of their shore camps was still moult-mottled brown and white.

The spring-swollen river carried the canoe to where it was headed in not many days. Already Deering's Point was covered with more wigwams, lean-tos, and temporary sleeping shelters made of hides awninged from overturned canoes, than there'd been last spring, and many more would be arriving. Some of the visitors had taken up residence in the big bark house Kelsey and Meyo had lived in for one winter. Meyo didn't much mind and it seemed Kelsey didn't either, since there was plenty of room and last winter had got him used to living in a big tent with other families in it. But then Meyo heard someone say, "Morning Wolf," and there—through the smoke of cooking fires and the bustle of big camp life and minnow-darting children—came her father.

Morning Wolf came close, then stopped, let out a sigh like his heart was too big for his chest and smiled misty-eyed, with one tear winding its way down one of the long, deep lines time had carved on his cheek. "Meyokwaiwin, and Misstopashish, and my grandson—"

"Daughter," Meyo squeezed out, throat tight.

"Of course," he looked down at the baby in her arms. "I should've known by the pretty face. What is her name?"

"Aurora," Meyo chopped in before Kelsey could answer.

A flicker of uncertainty crossed Meyo's father's face, then, "Ah, a white name. Well, she is half-white." He poked one gnarled finger at Wawatawin's nose and she wrapped her tiny fist around it. Meyo had to fight down an urge to jerk side-ways and get her baby out of his reach. She told herself that he was her father, as he had always been—and her baby's grandfather—but he looked different to her, and it wasn't just the wearing of two winters.

Morning Wolf turned his face to Kelsey. "So many things have happened, Misstopashish, since our eyes last met. Some things, if they had not happened, other things would not have happened. You seem happy with my daughter."

"I am."

"I heard you would be travelling to the salt water this spring, along with many canoes of people from many tribes. So I bundled together all the furs I and my brother trapped last winter, and joined up with some other hunters who are leaving their families for long enough to make the journey with you."

Meyo felt like she should be happy that her father want-ed to reconcile. Instead, it seemed to her that giving in to family feeling was just giving him something he could use. Back when it seemed more useful for Misstopashish to disappear and his friends at the salt water never know what had become of him, maybe never send a scout inland again, Morning Wolf was eager for that to happen. But now that Misstopashish was going back safely to the salt water and his powerful friends, Morning Wolf was eager to have him for a son by marriage.

Now her father's hooked nose didn't put Meyo in mind of Ohoomisew, the far-seeing owl, but of *Wendigo-kwekwes*, the downy, soft grey and white bird who looked as innocent as an oversized chickadee—until you saw him spike a tiny songbird to a thorn bush to hang there till he was ready to use it. Then you knew he was the Wendigo bird, the evil one. All that Morning Wolf's hook-beaked face needed to make the picture perfect was a black band across his eyes, and Meyo had seen him paint his face that way for a dog feast or to go on a raid.

But another voice inside her whispered that she was the evil one, for even thinking of thinking of him that way. He was her father and she owed him respect, not hatred. She told that voice she didn't hate him, and it wasn't just her grudge for the small things he'd said about her that night under the prairie stars—it was that she couldn't trust him. But then again...

She kept swinging back and forth, like a green poplar in a crosswind, in the days waiting for the time to go north from the Going North Place. At first she avoided him as much as she could, but there was one question she wanted to ask him. It was a question, though, that had to be asked when there was no one else around, just the two of them, and that grew more and more unlikely as more and more canoes arrived at Deering's Point.

Finally, one sunny afternoon, Meyo spotted Morning Wolf sitting by himself among the shore rocks, away from the bustle of the camp. She'd just finished feeding Wawatawin, so the wee one would happily sleep by herself for a while. Meyo could've carried the cradleboard along with her, but something made her want to keep Morning Wolf away from his granddaughter as much as possible.

Morning Wolf didn't look up till Meyo'd got very close—close enough to see what he was doing, and why he'd put himself by himself, away from all the liveliness. On a rock beside him was a moccasin sole with a hole in it big enough to see the grain of the rock. He was sewing a new sole onto the quillworked toe piece, concentrating hard on something he wasn't used to doing. When he did look up, he said, "Oh—wachiye, my daughter. See how clumsy-helpless a man is travelling without his wives and daughters? I would've asked you to mend it for me, but I know how busy a baby keeps its mother and father."

Meyo got straight to it. "Do you know that the morning on the prairie when you woke us before dawn and told us to gather our things quiet and leave without waking Misstopashish, I was already awake, and I already knew what you had planned?"

Her father's wrinkled eyes grew more wrinkled, like she was just being confusing.

"When you and Clawface and the others snuck away that night, to whisper about what to do about Misstopashish, I snuck along after you, and heard all that you said."

"Ah." Morning Wolf's face blossomed with understanding, and he nodded several times. "I see now what is troubling you, what's been troubling you for some while. A father can tell when his child is troubled, and when she is trying to keep her path from crossing his—as much as she can on this little scrap of land. I had thought I'd made it clear that I forgave you for disobeying me—some might say betraying me—but now I understand that when you went back to get Misstopashish it was not just a girl's sudden impulsiveness. You had planned it, and spied on me the night before, and lied to me all that morning.

"But," he spread his hands open, "if you had not done so, then Misstopashish would not be my son-in-law and we would not all be going with him to the whiteskins' fort to trade with his people. So again, and still, I forgive you." He smiled and reached a hand out for her shoulder.

Meyo's shoulder pulled itself back before his hand touched. She was still left with hearing Clawface say to Morning Wolf in fact: *"Misstopashish saved your daughter's life, and this is how you repay him?"* and her father replying: *"Her life isn't worth much to anybody, so there's nothing to repay."* But maybe there was something more to it she didn't understand, and maybe her father hadn't explained it to her because she hadn't made herself understood. She said, "I heard *every*thing you said that night."

"Yes, yes, I heard you say that. And did you hear me say, I forgive you, daughter?"

Meyo went away just as confused as before, though a different shade of confusion. Had he forgotten what he'd said that night? Or was he hoping she'd forgotten? Or maybe he meant that he'd only said that to Clawface because it was a useful thing to say at that moment and he hadn't really meant it? Was that supposed to make her feel safer—that he'd say anything to anybody if it got him what he wanted?

Or maybe he was just telling her that all that was long ago and far away made no difference now. Except it did.

XI

KELSEY HAD INCREASING REASON TO BELIEVE that his return to York Factory would bring a big upspring in The Company's annual returns. Deering's Point kept filling up with more wigwams and lean-tos, so much that they spilled out into the woods behind. Clawface kept telling him they should start north soon, before they lost the advantage of the spring runoff speeding their downstream journey. Kelsey kept stalling, "Just a few more days." None of the buffalo people had shown up yet, and it would naturally take them longer to get to Deering's Point from the plains.

It would also take them longer than the woodlands people to get home, so Kelsey expected Seven Stars and some Nakotas to show up any day. The Company's officers could make all the high-nosed jokes about "Indian Time" they wanted, everyone travelling to York Factory this spring knew they had to be back home by fall, and that the ice on the rivers would come back on its own time with no consideration of whether their canoes had passed or not.

Everyone except for Kelsey and his little family. But for some reason, when he tried to picture him and Meyo and Wawatawin wintering at York Factory it would only come out hazy-grey and indistinct, like distant figures moving in a fog. Well, if the last two years had taught him anything it should've been to not try picturing what was around the next bend in the path. What mattered at the moment was to get to York Factory with dozens of canoefuls of furs in his wake, including some of the Assinae Poets, and the journal of last summer's explorations in his pocket. That should raise "the boy Kelsey's" name in the higher offices of The Company in London, maybe even resonate as high as Sir Edward Deering.

On Deering's Point, things were complicated among Kelsey's new family and its offshoots. Whenever Meyo's father came near, Meyo said very little and her face turned into a mask carved from hard mahogany, even though she'd probably never seen mahogany. After a few days of that with no sign of change, Kelsey murmured to her in a moment alone, "Your father's just naturally doing what he needs to do to survive. The wind's turned. Back two autumns ago, I was something that might cause a disadvantage to him and his people—your people. Now, it's an advantage to him to have a whiteskin trader for a son-in-law."

"His people? *I* was his people—or one of them." She clamped her lips tight together as though getting ahold of herself, breathed through her nose a few times, then said in a flatter tone, "Yes, he will do anything to survive—do anything to anyone." Her eyes shifted to Aurora gurgling in the moss-lined niche by Meyo's side of the bed, the niche that travelled with them wherever they made their bed—all it needed was a few handfuls of moss and something to prop against it.

Kelsey didn't know whether that glance at Wawatawin had anything to do with what Meyo'd just said, or whether it was just the clockwork magnet that drew a mother's eyes to check on her baby every half hour, or half minute. He did know he'd said all he could say and that Meyo and Morning Wolf had years more history between them than Meyo and Misstopashish. Even though Kelsey hadn't had much experience with family life, he had a strong suspicion that getting stuck between a father and daughter wasn't a smart place to be. So he went back to just being stuck between everyone else's urge to get paddling north and his own urge to wait until Seven Stars and the buffalo people came paddling around the bend above Deering's Point.

Finally somebody did arrive from the prairie country. But it was just a lone paddler in a small canoe, and he wasn't one of the buffalo people, just a man of the woodlands who sometimes travelled with them. He brought a message for Misstopashish, and a present from the man who'd sent the message.

The present was a pair of baby-sized moccasins decorated on the toe pieces with seven little silver-coloured beads. The message from Seven Stars was that there had been some more killings, so he didn't trust that the woodland people would let his people pass safely through to the salt water this year. But if Misstopashish's chief at the salt water would send Seven Stars a piece of tobacco this year, Seven Stars would bring many canoes full of beaver pelts next year. Enclosed with the tiny moccasins was a present for Misstopashish's chief, the Governor: a pipe made of blue-veined marble rubbed so thin that the light of a tobacco coal inside it would glow right through.

Kelsey had no trouble believing that the messenger had repeated exactly what Seven Stars had said to him, or damn close. With no written language to fall back on, the Indians had an uncanny ability to remember a message word for word, especially when they had good reason to expect a present for delivering it. Kelsey gave the man two axe heads and a knife and he went away happy.

What Kelsey did have trouble with was understanding the reason behind the message. Why would next year be any safer than this year? Maybe the buffalo people never intended to make the journey, ever, and were just trying to get as many presents as they could in exchange for promises that would always be "next year."

Kelsey mulled it over with Meyo, and as usual their two different ways of thinking came up with some kind of sense out of the puzzle. So far all that the buffalo people knew first-hand of the white traders was that only one of them, and a very junior one at that, had travelled to the prairie. That might be just a one-time thing. But if the traders sent tobacco all the way from the salt water to the plains this year, that would seem more of an ongoing connection. And if next year Seven Stars could tell the woodlands people he'd been sent tobacco by the headman of the traders they got their guns and knives from, so was travelling under his protection, the men of the woods might think twice about ambush and robbery.

Whether or not that was exactly the thinking behind the message, or maybe something else that Kelsey and Meyo couldn't think of between them, there was clearly no point in waiting any longer before starting north. As with last year, most of the women and children and some of the men would stay behind at Deering's Point, but there would still be several times more canoes travelling to York Factory together than ever had before.

Kelsey was propping his rifle safely into the lead canoe when he saw Morning Wolf approaching as though he would naturally be travelling in the same canoe as his daughter, son-in-law and granddaughter. Meyo stepped in front of him and said, "You're not coming with us."

Morning Wolf stopped and said, "Oh. Not enough room in your canoe?"

"I mean you're not coming with *us*." She waved her arm out to include the whole fleet of canoes. "If you wait here till the canoes come back, then you will still get better trading for your furs than you would in our home woods, where the white man's things have to pass through many hands before they get there."

"You can't tell me where I can or can't go."

"This man," Meyo pointed at Kelsey, "saved my life from two bears while you were busy gambling. And then you left him alone to die. Why shouldn't he just kill you now?"

Actually, Kelsey could think of several reasons why he shouldn't, but decided not to butt in.

Morning Wolf raised his voice and looked like he was about to raise his hand. "I am your father, girl!"

A strange, unnatural calm settled over Kelsey. Or maybe it was more natural than the world he'd been brought up in, because he felt the muscles in his neck and shoulders going loose and easy where he hadn't even known they'd been tense. Beyond Morning Wolf's shoulder he saw Clawface bland-faced leaning on his paddle, like a harnessed horse waiting for whatever was holding things up to get done with so they could get moving.

Kelsey's strange calm came from realizing that if he just casually pulled one of the pistols out of his belt and shot Morning Wolf dead, none of the hundreds of people around would say anything about it except, "Damn stupid of Morning Wolf to start a fight with a man who had two loaded guns close at hand." Maybe Meyo would feel sad about it after the fact, or maybe not, she was pretty mad.

Morning Wolf looked at Kelsey and then turned and walked away without looking at his daughter again.

The canoe they were travelling in was a big one, with four paddlers besides Kelsey and Meyo. Clawface paddled from the bow, since he'd travelled this route more than anyone and knew what to look out for where. Some nights the fleet had to camp on both sides of the river, to find enough open ground for all the people and canoes. That became less of a problem as they got farther north-east and the trees grew smaller and farther apart. Eventually there were no trees at all, except wind-twisted, little scraggly things scattered here and there. The Land of Little Sticks, the Indians called it.

Partway through one morning, Kelsey smelled salt water. Clawface looked back and they nodded at each other. Soon York Factory came into view. After two years of seeing no human construction bigger than a wigwam or a tipi, Kelsey had some idea of the impression the fort must make on the Indians, with its tall log walls hundreds of paces wide. Meyo said, "Is that what happened to all the trees?" and Kelsey laughed.

His laugh was drowned out by a clap of thunder from below the sky. Grey smoke puffed out of the fort wall facing the river and the canoes. Meyo let out a squawk and there were a few other nervous sounds from those who'd never heard a cannon before. Kelsey knew it was nothing to be alarmed about; the cannon boom had only been a blank charge fired by way of a salute, and anyway most of the fort's guns were mounted on the front wall pointed towards the bay, in case the French came calling.

Then again, maybe it was the people inside the fort who were a bit nervous, and the cannon salute had been meant as a blusterish warning. The sentries on the walls had never seen so many hunter-warriors coming down the river at once.

As the prow of the canoe neared the riverbank, Clawface jumped out into the water and took hold of the gunwale. All of the paddlers did the same in turn, so the front part of the canoe raised up while the stern was still afloat and they could lift it forward instead of dragging its birch bark bottom across the rocks and gravel of the shore. As the rest of the canoes were beached and their crews headed toward the camp of Home Guard Indians to scout out places to put up their own wigwams, Kelsey said to Meyo, "You and I aren't going there, we're going *there*," and pointed toward the fort.

Aurora had somehow managed to stay asleep through all the noise and excitement. Meyo called to a woman from one of the other canoes who had a suckling baby of her own, and left Wawatawin with her in case she woke up hungry before Meyo got back. As Kelsey and Meyo climbed the riverbank rise toward the fort, he could hear her breathing becoming short and sharp and shallow, and it wasn't because the rise was steep. He hooked his arm through hers and said, "It's just a camp like any other, except it's made of wood and don't move. The men inside it walk on two legs the same as any other men."

As Kelsey and Meyo neared the tightly closed gates, a head and shoulders appeared above the pencil-sharpened log tops of the palisades. The man was silhouetted against the sun spreading its light through a grey film of cloud, so Kelsey couldn't make out any features. But even if he could've, Kelsey wasn't sure he'd recognize one of his old messmates, or maybe an officer whose boots he'd polished, after so much time and distance.

The man above the gates called down, "Kelsey? Is that really you?"

"How many blonde Indians do you know?"

"Well, I thought it must be you, so I've sent for the Governor."

There was a moment of waiting, during which Kelsey had time to notice the sounds, or lack of them—no voices but those of men inside the fort going about their business, and a few squawking seagulls. Kelsey recollected that the woods or meadows around any Indian village were alive with songbirds twittering about their day, but the only birds who came within sight or sound of York Factory were the gulls and ravens who lived on human garbage.

Another silhouette appeared above the palisade beside the sentry's. This one was taller and its outline included the shape of a curled wig and a tricorne hat. The Governor called down, "Kelsey, lad! Ye're back safe, excellent! Gone far, have ye?"

"Yes, sir," he patted the moosehide shoulder pouch hanging beside his right hip, and the oilcloth-wrapped notebook inside it. "And brought back a written record of it." Kelsey was finding he had to struggle some with English after not speaking it or hearing it for two years—except for bits and pieces with Meyo, and that was hardly conversation fit for a governor. He had to think twice about whether the tall man above the gates was the governor or the okimaw.

"Bloody marvellous, lad. First rate. We'll have a lot to talk about. I'll have 'em open the gates enough for ye to come in."

"Thank you, sir. We'll be glad to come in."

The Governor—whose silhouette had turned as though to call down an order to the gatekeeper—stopped and turned to look down at Kelsey again. "Ye misunderstood me, Kelsey. I meant of course 'ye' singular, not plural. Surely ye can't've been gone long enough to forget...? The Company has an ironclad policy that no, um, people of the country, are to be allowed inside our forts. *Ye* can come in, of course, and more than welcome. But not...*she*."

Kelsey could feel Meyo shrinking beside him. He knew she'd picked up enough English to know what was going on, at least the gist. Looking up at the silhouette of the governor, he realized how much had changed since the last time the great man had deigned to speak with "the boy Kelsey." One thing that hadn't changed was that anything more than a mile inland of the bay still might as well be the surface of the moon so far as the Governor of York Factory knew, or anyone else in The Company of Adventurers Trading Into Hudson's Bay. But now little Henry Kelsey had travelled hundreds of miles out onto the surface of the moon, and come back to tell them what was there. If he would.

The other change Kelsey realized was that now he had a choice. He could go back to Deering's Point with Meyo and Wawatawin and live out the rest of his life among the Indians. Whether or not The Company still owned him by indenture would mean absolutely nothing, just as it meant nothing that The Company technically owned all the very useful things in the two caches Meyo could find for him again. What was The Company going to do, send bailiffs after him? There were probably some things he'd miss about civilization, and some things he wouldn't.

Kelsey called up to the Governor, "Well, if *we* can't come in, then I guess we'll have to go back somewhere we *can* go."

Kelsey turned around and Meyo, with her arm linked in his, naturally wheeled with him.

"Wait!"

Kelsey stopped and turned around again, Meyo turning with him.

"Demmit, Kelsey, I...Ye can't just...That is to say... Oh bloody hell. Open the gates!"

Author's Note

ONE THING THAT CAN ANNOY ME about historical novels is when I don't have a clue whether the writer tried to stick to historical facts, or just used some historical names for publicity value and then made up whatever s/he felt like making up. So I try not to annoy my readers that way. So I'll tell you right here that my prime directive is I can make up stuff between historically documented facts, but I can't mess with the facts.

However, ye olde "historically documented facts" can be slippery. For instance: as I hinted in the front note, the "facts" about just how old/young Henry Kelsey was when he travelled west from Hudson Bay in 1690 - 92. Various history texts say he was born in 1670, *c.* 1670 or *c.* 1667. But I'd always had the feeling Kelsey was a teenager when he went west.

Teenage boys (and girls) got handed a lot of heavy lifting in those days. Radisson was about sixteen when he got hired to guide a group of Jesuit missionaries into Iroquois country. The HBC records from around 1690 do refer to "the boy Kelsey," and "a very active Lad Delighting much in Indians Company." And an HBC man a generation later, relating what he'd heard from the old fellas, wrote: "A little boy, Henry Kelsey..."

But none of that added up with the Kelsey birth dates given by historians of my generation and the previous generation. Well, I hate to have to be the one to tell you, but sometimes some historians can be a bit...lazy. Or maybe a nicer way to put it would be: a bit too respectful of their elders. A historian of my generation might just copy as fact a date given by a historian of the previous generation, who actually had simply copied it from an elder historian, who... Doesn't always happen that way, but it happens. So I traced it back down the line to the original research.

Turns out the original researcher said clearly that the only old documents she could find that might tell us anything about Henry Kelsey's birthdate are only connected to him by a stretch of maybes. First off, Kelsey lived out his last years in Greenwich, England and died there, so *maybe* he was born there. A "John Kelsey, mariner," probably a sea captain, died there in 1674 and his will mentions his eldest son Henry, so *maybe* that's our Henry.

The problem with those maybes is that there's no date given for that Henry's birth—not at all unusual in those days for there to be no record of someone's birth, or the records to disappear over the centuries—but the second son was definitely baptized in 1668, which means older brother Henry couldn't've been born any later than 1667. Even the Dictionary of Canadian Biography, which understandably likes to be able to put dates to things, admits that "b. 1667" would make our Henry Kelsey a bit old to sign on as a cabin boy in 1684, where the HBC records first mention him. And I'll add that the firstborn sons of middle class families didn't usually become indentured servants, one step up from out and-out slavery, and HBC records show that's how Kelsey started with The Company.

So the theory that "the boy Kelsey" was born *c.* 1667 is highly theoretical. One thing that isn't theoretical is that Kelsey was and is a fairly common name throughout the British Isles—good chance dozens of Henry Kelseys were born in the late 1600s.

As for the notion that our Henry Kelsey was born in 1670, the only reason I've ever been able to find for that is somebody back when thought it'd be cute if Kelsey'd been born the same year as the Hudson's Bay Company, and some other people just copied it down. Yeah, that's how official history happens sometimes.

So why this assumption that Kelsey must've been in his twenties when he went west? Frankly, prejudice. A lot of history gets written by stuffy old guys, even older'n me, who assume that nobody's capable of doing anything until they're at least old enough to vote. Well, like I said about Radisson... Makes more sense to me that The Company would choose a teenager to send out on possible suicide missions.

The 18th century HBC man who wrote of: "A little boy, Henry Kelsey," is where we get the story of the two grizzly bears attacking Kelsey's "Indian companion," Kelsey killing one and then the second one when it turned on him, which earned Kelsey the nickname Misstopashish or Little Giant. The story might've got muddled in a few details, but the word 'misstopashish' gives good reason to believe it's essentially true. That same writer also recorded the traditional story of what happened when Kelsey showed up at the gates of York Factory with his "Indian wife," which is one of several reasons to believe there truly was a person like the one I've christened Meyokwaiwin... But we'll get to that.

Back to the name "Misstopashish," and why it lends credibility to that 18th century writer's grizzly story. It's very close to *mistapoa*, the Cree word for "giant" in the mid-nineteenth century Cree/English Dictionary sitting on my desk, which also says that one way to say "little-something" is to add on "isis" or "is" or "itis." Mid-nineteenth century is about as far back as English/Cree translations go, and languages and pronunciation have been known to change a bit over time. So do tribal areas. The people Kelsey encountered in the northern woodlands and grasslands were *probably* a mixture of what we now call Cree and Assiniboine, with maybe a dash of Ojibway on the side.

There's pretty good evidence that there actually once was a translation dictionary written long before the mid-nineteenth century, written by... Henry Kelsey. In 1710 the HBC Governor in London wrote to Kelsey: "We have sent you your dixianary Printed..." Forty years later a retired fur trader wrote: "I was told that (Kelsey) wrote a vocabulary of the Indian language, and that the Company had ordered it to be suppressed." Why would the Hudson's Bay Company want it buried? Well, if anyone who could read English could communicate with Indian trappers, then any Tom, Dick or Harry could go into the fur trade business. "Competition" was a four-letter word to ye olde HBC.

If Kelsey's "dixionary" had survived we might be able to translate the strongest piece of evidence that there was someone like Meyo in Henry Kelsey's life. In late December of 1696, four-and-a-half years since he came back to York Factory from the west, his daily journal suddenly breaks away from weather and business and he writes:

Arrabeck or indian language of hudsons bay:

Then there are half a dozen lines in what might be something vaguely like Cree, maybe, but no one's ever been able to decipher it. Seventeenth century *English* spelling was eccentric enough, so an Englishman's spelling of an obscure dialect of a foreign language... But there is at least some clue toward what those "Arrabeck" words were about, because on New Year's Eve Kelsey added in English, on the opposite page beside those half-dozen lines:

A pleasant fancy of old time
which made me write in an unknown
tongue because counsel is kept best in
one single Breast

Below that he wrote in smaller letters *vale*, which is kind of a poetic way of saying "farewell" but more so, the same word we get "valedictorian" from.

There are a few more bits of evidence that there was someone like Meyo in Kelsey's life. Part of the July 23rd entry in his 1691 prairie journal is: "...so I gave him some powder & an Order to receive some shott of such a woman..." which seems to say pretty clearly that there was a specific woman Kelsey trusted to take charge of his goods while he was scouting ahead. Like that incident, many others in the story you've just read—Kelsey waking up alone and terrified in the middle of nowhere, his birchbark & charcoal letter to the Governor, his burnt gunstock, etc. etc.—were taken straight out of Kelsey's journals, or the written reminiscences of people who heard his stories in the long winter nights on Hudson Bay.

As for exactly which First Nation Meyokwaiwin and the others belonged to, and who exactly were the Naywatamee Poets, etc.—good luck to anyone trying to figure that out. "Assinae Poets" does sound a lot like Assiniboine, but other than that... Tribes and nations were a lot more fluid than we're led to believe, and that doesn't just apply to North American aboriginals—when I was researching the Highland

Clearances for another book, I found Clan Sutherland chockful of MacPhersons, MacLeods and MacBeths. And all the tribes and territories Kelsey met up with changed immensely a few decades later with the coming of the horse to the northern plains. Even if that change hadn't jumbled everything, the last few weeks of Kelsey's westward journal—August/September of 1691, before he settled in for the winter—is a confusing multiple ping pong of Naywatames, Nayhaythaways, Stone Indians, Assinae Poets and—just in case we're not confused enough—some shadowy new tribe he called the Mountain Poets. By that point in his travels, Kelsey was just taking it as it comes, jot down a few notes and see what bounces down the road tomorrow.

A version of Kelsey's travel journals was printed by The Company to help prove to Parliament they were fulfilling their mandate to explore North America and search out a Northwest Passage. The original handwritten documents disappeared after Kelsey died and only reappeared in 1926. They'd been shuffled from attic to attic for two hundred years, sorta like Great Grandma's photo album.

The weirdest thing about "The Kelsey Papers" is there's no journal for 1690, the first year he travelled west. Instead there are three pages of rhyming couplets written a few years later, sort of "The Ballad of My Summer Vacation." Some of it's cute, some of it's informative, some of it tells The Company that if this "journal" isn't good enough for them they can stuff it, and some of it's obviously only there because he needed a rhyme for the next line. Some historians have assumed that this ballady summary means Kelsey didn't keep a journal in 1690. Me, I don't think so. Kelsey kept a daily journal of his trip north in 1689, and of his further travels west in 1691, and for several years after he got back

to York Factory. Why not 1690? I think he did keep a journal in 1690, but something happened to it. What exactly is
anybody's guess—could've been a boating accident, could've
been the way I told it in this story.

Along those same lines, it's been assumed and repeated
that Kelsey spent the first winter of his journey, 1690-91, with
the plains tribes, as he did the winter of 1691-92. But there's
absolutely no evidence that he didn't go back to Deering's
Point and spent that first winter there, and a few reasons to
think he did.

Oh, one thing I did consciously fudge was York Factory,
which "the boy Kelsey" would've called York Fort. It wasn't
till a while later that The Company started calling its main
posts York Factory, Moose Factory, etc. Personally, I think
they only made the change to get gullible young children
traumatically teased for believing that's where the HBC
manufactured moose, but I'm over it now. Anyway, there
are so many other York Forts and Fort Yorks dotted through
Canadian history, I thought I'd save confusion.

Henry Kelsey did eventually become Governor of York
Factory and of all the English forts on Hudson Bay, which the
French continued to raid and capture from time to time, twice
taking Kelsey prisoner. On one of his trips back to England, he
married an Englishwoman in East Greenwich. What became
of Kelsey's "Indian wife," no one knows. I think she and Kelsey
inevitably ran up against the same dilemma as Harrison Ford
and Kelley McGillis in *Witness*: there was no in-between
world. It wasn't till a hundred years after Kelsey died that the
Red River Settlement made a place where HBC men and their
native wives and children could live out their lives together.

If Meyokwaiwin (or whatever her real name was) did go
back to her own people, she likely had a hoard of practical

treasures close to hand. Kelsey's 1692 journal doesn't mention digging up the barrel they'd buried in 1691, the barrel filled with gunpowder and axe heads and other goodies. And although I invented the canvas-wrapped cache hung in a pine tree in 1690, there's nothing to say it didn't exist.

While I'm talking about Meyo again, I should mention that her relatively offhanded, offstage childbirth isn't something I pulled out of a hat, so to speak. Many very reliable witnesses recorded incidents like riding along with an Indian band that included a very pregnant woman who suddenly said: "Oh, it's time! The rest of you go on ahead, I'll catch up with you." And an hour or so later she and her new baby did. There were a lot of different theories of why native women's birthing was generally so different from white women's, but no question of the fact.

Another thing I definitely didn't pull out of a hat was Henry Kelsey's affinity for the "benighted savages" of the wilderness. When he became a fort governor, on at least two occasions he had men flogged for "mistreatment of ye Indians," and probably did the flogging himself. His writings are pretty much just-business, not much room for reading his character. But enough slips through to get a pretty good handle on the guy. For one thing, he wasn't afraid to admit being afraid: *"And once yt in my travels I was left behind, Which struck fear & terror into me."* And every now and then there's a glimpse of a slightly quirky attitude that doesn't quite fit with the prevailing views of the world, like his description of the grizzly bear: *"He is mans food & he makes food of man."*

In 1981 Kelsey was memorialized in Stan Rogers's *Northwest Passage*, sort of. The line in the studio-recorded song is: "In the footsteps of brave Kelso where his sea of flowers began." It seems at the time Mr. Rogers wasn't entirely sure of the pronunciation, and once they'd got the whole multi-verse, a cappella, harmonized epic safely on tape once... Oh well, it's the thought that counts.

No one actually dared follow in the footsteps of brave Kelsey/Kelso until almost half a century later. The next European eyes to see the sea of flowers were the La Vérendryes' in the 1730s. Forty years gives maybe some idea of what a mad venture "the boy Kelsey" set off on alone in 1690.

Well, one last thing, and it's a bit of a strange one. Strange things sometimes happen when you're writing about real people who are long dead. On the day I finished the first draft of the last chapter of this book, I read the chapter aloud to my wife (I always foist first drafts on her, to see if anything clunks or doesn't, then I leave her alone for the second or third drafts or whatever). That done, I set the chapter aside and picked up the day's newspaper to have a bit of a read with my lunch. The paper runs a little "Today In History" column which I sometimes glance at but not always. That day I did and saw:

Also on this date in:

1691, Henry Kelsey of the Hudson's Bay Co. was the first white man to see what is now Saskatchewan.